MONSTER FEATURES

USA TODAY BESTSELLING AUTHOR
N GRAY

VINCI
BOOKS

"Whoever fights monsters should see to it that in the process he does not become a monster.
And if you gaze long enough into an abyss, the abyss will gaze back into you."

— *Friedrich Nietzsche*

Vinci Books

vinci-books.com

Published by Vinci Books Ltd in 2026

1

Copyright © N Gray 2020

The EU GPSR authorised representative is Logos Europe, 9 rue Nicolas
Poussion, 17000 La Rochelle, France
contact@logoseurope.eu

By N Gray

Shifter Days, Vampire Nights & Demons in Between

Twisted

Lady Hawk and Her Mountain Man

Hidden Shifter

Wolf

Wolf Retreat

Night Hunter

The Fixer

Kai

Lee

Flynn

Jude

More from N Gray writing as Natalie Michaels

Steve Campbell Psychological Suspense Thrillers

The Last Girl

The Bone Forest

The White Dahlia

I See You

Death in the City

More from N Gray writing as SD Syns

The Diaries

Red Lace Diaries

www.ngraybooks.com

ONE

Ravenous

PART 1

ERIK
Norway, Circa 960 AD

Erik stopped beside a tree and watched his father enter the chieftain's home where all the men had gathered. They were about to decide their family's fate, a decision that could result in their entire family moving far from Norway.

"Do you know why they blame your father?" Erik recognized his friend's voice without having to turn to answer Torsten.

"They think my father killed three men."

"Yours and mine."

Erik hadn't known Torsten's father was involved. He turned to look at his friend, his face stained with tears and dirt. "I thought it was only my father?"

Torsten shook his head. "Mother says Father helped. It's all because of the land they farm on, and the chieftain's cousin wanted it—"

"And they fought?"

"Yes." Torsten nodded, wiping away a stray tear.

"And three men lost their lives because of it. And they're blaming our fathers because the chieftain's cousin wanted our land?"

Torsten nodded again.

Erik rarely got angry, but since turning ten, things easily set him off. His anger flared to life the moment he had found out his dad was in trouble, and now again, his anger was as ripe as any adult's, knowing his best friend's father was also involved. If he could, he would grab an axe and charge the chieftain's cousin—put an end to this fight once and for all. If the cousin was no longer around, then the chieftain wouldn't have to defend him all the time. Or send hard-working men away.

A loud noise erupted from the chieftain's home as men screamed their votes. It was unanimous. Erik's father exited the house with his head down and shoulders rounded forward.

Erik left his friend and ran to his father, who pushed him away. "Not now, Erik."

"What happened, Father?"

"Pack your things, son. We leave at dawn." His father's reply was curt, and he pushed past Erik.

Erik stopped dead—his body numb, his mind clouded over. For a boy entering manhood, he felt stuck. This land was his birthplace, and now they had to leave because of a vote. That something as small as one vote by each of the men he had grown up to admire could cause so much heartache. And that all the men wanted his father, their family, gone. Now they had to travel across the rough seas in search of unknown land. They had heard of many families moving to Iceland. Perhaps it would be an adventure, or their demise.

Torsten approached him. But before he could mutter anything, Erik screamed and punched Torsten in the face. Anger and frustration coursed through his veins, and his face matched his fiery hair. Torsten nursed his aching cheek, fell to the ground and cried.

Shocked by what he'd done, Erik blinked back tears and ran home. When he opened the door to their house, his mother was crying into a cloth, and his father was packing.

———

The next morning, they were waiting near the boats with what they could carry. Everything else they would source when they arrived at their new land. Erik's father brought the rest of their possessions as Torsten and his family approached.

Erik dropped his belongings near his mother and ran to his friend. He had to make amends for his behavior yesterday. Torsten was his one and only best friend; they were like blood brothers, and it was awful of Erik to take out his frustration on Torsten. He regretted his action more than anything.

"That's close enough, boy." Torsten's father stopped Erik from coming closer with a finger to his chest.

"I would like to own up for my behavior and apologize to my friend." Erik's chin trembled as he composed his emotions.

Torsten bit his lip. Tears welled in his eyes when he looked at his father. "It's all right."

His father nodded and carried their belongings to the boat they would share with Erik's family.

"I'm sorry, Torsten. I should not have taken out my

anger on you. Do you forgive me?" Erik averted his eyes and stared at the mud at their feet.

Torsten dropped his bag and hugged Erik.

"Only women hug," Erik's dad said from behind them and chuckled. "Come, boys, we must go now before something else happens."

The boys hugged one last time, carried their belongings to the boat then helped their fathers pack the rest of their things, so they could set sail.

Two other families were aboard the boat; four men had been exiled after last night's voting for various deeds that some may not think warranted such hefty sentences. But no one went against their chieftains' word, as that would be treacherous and dangerous. That person could be killed, along with his entire family.

Now the men and their families had to leave Norway for Iceland.

The voyage they were about to embark on could take as little as three days if the weather was favorable, but, if the wind was against them, it would take them longer.

Torsten and Erik sat beside each other and watched Norway become smaller until it winked out completely, and the ocean surrounded them.

There were stories of monsters in rough seas, and Erik wondered whether they would encounter them on their voyage. He had only been out to sea once with his father, but that was only a day's trip, and they were back before dark. Now they would travel all day, all night, for at least three days. He wasn't looking forward to it.

Their first evening at sea was uneventful, and Erik was grateful. If anything happened to the boat and threw them overboard, he could only swim for a short while. He shoved down the daunting thoughts where they belonged and tried to think of other, more pleasant things.

Erik and Torsten played games with the other children around their age while the adults spoke in low tones. No doubt they were discussing what had happened at the vote the day before and the land of their future. Erik could see his mother was glad one of the exiled families owned a boat for them all to leave on. That's what Erik had heard when he passed them; when they saw him, they spoke quietly again.

Their meals comprised of porridge and dried fruit, or perhaps buttermilk and bread, while in the evenings, they ate fish or meat stewed with vegetables. Their mothers also gave them dried fruit with honey as a sweet treat.

Two other kids and one mother experienced sickness aboard the boat, but, after the third day, they were fine. Erik was glad the movement of the sea didn't affect him as badly, although Torsten was slightly ill the first day and gave him his buttermilk.

Late afternoon on the fourth day, thunder cracked in the distance. Both boys' heads shot up at the gloomy clouds looming above them. The air smelled of rain while the wind caressed their faces and sprayed them with sea water. They were blessed to have great weather during their time at sea, even though the winds had been against them. But now, chaos erupted on the boat as the adults moved about, locking down items, closing latches, and ensuring everyone was safe.

The seas darkened around the boat, and the waves splashed over them—but not enough to worry the adults, yet. Erik and Torsten sat beside each other and held on as the boat rocked. Lightning struck in the distance, and the light flashed brightly enough for them to cover their faces.

Erik's arms pebbled at the cool breeze and pulled on his fur coat.

Erik glanced behind him when a strange sound caught his attention—a soft lullaby with soft music, a sound he'd never heard before. It was poetic and beautiful. His brows furrowed. It was not the sound he had expected out here during a storm. When he glimpsed his surroundings, the music stopped. Above them, the cumulonimbus clouds neared, bringing with it thunder and lightning.

Erik stood when the music started again. The song reminded him of a rhyme his mother had sung to him when he was young and had struggled to fall asleep. The water rippled. The waves splashed against the boat and sprayed salty water in his face. Licking his lips, he squinted at something in the rippling black water. The objected grew bigger the closer it came to the surface.

The water had calmed enough for him to grip the side of the boat and safely lean overboard to see what it was. The clouds covered the sun and helped him see the object in the water clearer, and she smiled at him.

The youthful woman was at least five years older than him. Her skin was pale, eyes the color of cerulean seas with a cloudy undertone that shimmered, reminding him of mother-of-pearl his mother had shown him once. The woman smiled again and beckoned him to follow her. He shook his head and peered over his shoulder at the adults now bracing themselves for the approaching storm.

He turned to the woman, and her face was completely out of the water. He saw more of her and felt his cheeks heat and something stir in the pit of his stomach. The woman dove through the water, revealing her glimmering scales the same color as her eyes. The enticing lullaby sounded again, and Erik had the urge to dive into the water and join the young maiden within the deepest waters where he would remain. If only he could touch her just once, then he could belong to her, to be hers, and to love her forever.

"Erik! What are you doing?" Erik recognized his father's loud voice behind him, but it sounded far away. A hand gripped his shoulder, and it felt like a bubble popped in his face, and his thoughts became his own again.

He swallowed hard, turned to his father then back to the murky water, but the woman was gone.

"What's out there, boy?" his father asked in a tone that made his skin crawl and made him feel worthless and stupid.

"It's n-nothing. J-Just a dolphin I think."

The look in his father's eyes told him he knew it was a lie but didn't call him out. "Brace yourself, boy, or you'll swim with the fish soon enough." He let go of Erik, handed him a rope to hold onto and returned to his mother.

"I saw something too. It was a woman, wasn't it?" Torsten whispered beside him. He too was leaning over the edge at the dark waters.

"We don't know what we saw. It could just be the sea air or salty water that's making our brains see things."

"I know what I saw, and that was not the kraken nor the sea serpent. It was a woman with a fish's tail."

"You—"

The gentle music interrupted Erik's words. Only this time, both boys peered over the edge. He knew his friend was seeing what he was seeing. She wasn't something from their stories; she was something new and inviting. He wanted to dive into the water and spend eternity with her. He loved her and wanted to give her everything he owned. He felt Torsten move forward, both their faces near the water. If the boat were to rock, they would be underwater.

The woman swam to the surface with her hands outstretched, about to grab hold of them, when something gripped his collar and dragged both boys to the center of the boat.

"No!" Erik's dad said to the boys. "Do not look at her again, and, if you hear the music, cover your ears." He peered over the side of the boat. "It will end badly for both of you. She's not what she makes herself out to be. She invades your thoughts and plants others, making you want to dive in and be with her. I've lost too many honorable men. I can't lose you too." He pulled Erik into an embrace. "She won't stop until she gets one of you. If you hear her again, ignore her. Now come help us."

Erik and Torsten nodded sheepishly and helped their parents prepare the boat for the storm. Just as they finished securing everything and ensuring they too wouldn't go overboard, the storm hit them as if the gods themselves were angry at their departure, that the gods were punishing them for what their fathers had done to protect their families.

All four families huddled together to brace for impact. Rain lashed down on them, and wind blew drops with such force it felt as though it sliced their skin. The boat rocked from the gigantic waves, as if the kraken itself was moving beneath them. The women prayed while the men kept everyone safe.

Torsten's father stood to steer the boat from the approaching rocks. The same music filled the air as the storm pummeled down on them.

Erik glanced at Torsten with knowing eyes. She had returned, but they both stayed seated. They huddled together and braced for the storm.

Everyone stayed awake during the night while the storm

hit them from all sides. As the storm subsided at daybreak, they fell asleep from exhaustion.

Erik woke when water splashed on his face. Sitting up, he saw tall mountainous figures sticking out of the water that resembled trolls. On his left was Iceland, dark land covered in white. Snow fell gently around them. He shivered from the frosty weather and damp clothing and found a dry fur coat to pull on. The rocking of the boat was smooth as they sailed along the coastline.

Soon they arrived near a beach, the sand as dark as night. Shouting from afar woke everybody in the boat. People ran on loose wooden planks.

"Welcome to Reykjavík," someone said near their boat with a broad smile and friendly face.

Everybody sat upright. They had reached Iceland and somehow had steered in the right direction—right to the village and near the wooden pier as if the gods had helped them during their fight with earth's elements and the lady in the water.

Everyone moved about the boat until Torsten's mother's scream pierced the air. She pointed at something in the water behind the boat. Everybody went to see what it was.

Tied to the rope behind the boat was Torsten's father; his beaten and bloated body was face down. They had chewed off his left leg, and a crab emerged from a hole in his back. Torsten's mother fainted in Erik's father's arms, who gently laid her down then untied the body. It was now his responsibility to look after her family as well. It was his fault they were there with them.

Although this was devastating to Torsten and his family, Erik knew that through their father's sacrifice and good fortune, it was what had led them to their new home on a strange, mysterious land.

The villagers were accommodating and welcoming and helped build each family a new home.

A week after they had arrived, they had settled into their new homes on Iceland.

Torsten's family lived next door, and his mother had already started seeing their new chieftain's son, who was young enough to be Torsten's much older brother.

One day, Erik watched his father chop wood with an axe and then chopped the smaller blocks into manageable pieces for their fire. Once done, he called over Erik. "Erik, one day you'll be a skilled leader."

"How do you know?"

"I have seen it." He ruffled Erik's red hair and kept his hand on Erik's head. "I think it's the fire in you." He laughed then continued in a serious tone. "Things are out there we need to be careful of." He stared at Erik for a heartbeat to punctuate his words.

"The lady in the water?"

"Yes, her and so many others I have not even seen." He let go of Erik and grabbed his axe. "The visions I've seen showed me you'll continue on many travels. You'll lead your people to greater discoveries, but you need to remember one thing."

Erik edged closer to his father, eager to listen.

"Keep your men safe from harm. You've only seen one monster, but there are many more we have yet to encounter."

Ravenous

PART 2

TORSTEN
Greenland, Circa 982 AD

Erik glanced over his shoulder at Torsten, his eyes wide and filled with panic. But Torsten knew his friend would never admit his true feelings—that's not what berserkers did. He and Erik had been best friends since they were young, and he had followed Erik to Greenland where they would fight together in many raids.

Now their boats were sinking, following a terrifying storm they had just emerged from, and, even though their land was up ahead, they were on the wrong side. Their village was on the other side. They had never been to this side of Greenland before, where the mountains were rough, high, and spine-chilling from where Torsten stood in the boat, the water already knee high.

They were sinking fast.

"Torsten, we need to swim to shore." Erik threw the

oars into the sea and lifted himself off the side of the boat and into the water.

Torsten nodded to the rest of the men staring up at him. They all held that same expression—concerned and frightened. Torsten grabbed the jug of mead they were passing around, enjoyed large gulps until he felt heat in his chest, on his neck, and cheeks then gave it to Njal. Once everyone was warm from the mead, they packed their bags with as much equipment, food, and drink as they could carry. They tucked their axes into their belts and jumped into the unknown.

Torsten's legs were already numb from the chilly water. As he sunk the rest of his body into the icy waters, his chest rose and fell, then he stopped breathing until he got used to the sting of the ocean. The shore wasn't a great distance, so he didn't have that far to swim. But it would be a struggle.

Cries sounded from the other men as they jumped to their deaths; some could swim, others not so well, and they sunk to the bottom and on their way to Valhalla.

"Hurry!" Erik yelled from shore, frantically waving his arms. He said something else, but Torsten couldn't hear him as his head dipped underwater.

As Torsten reached the surface, a wave crashed on top of him, knocking out his breath. He waded in the water to keep from drowning and sucked in air in short, quick bursts before being dragged down again.

A weight on his ankle pulled. Realizing something was holding him, Torsten opened his eyes underwater, which stung, and all he saw was the deepest black of the water. Whatever held on, he couldn't see it properly; it looked like it had a long tentacle or two, but Torsten couldn't be sure. He could only open his eyes for brief periods of time, and each time, the monster moved just out of sight.

Torsten's heart thundered, and his lungs burned as he held onto his last breath. Torsten would die if he didn't do something, and quickly. The thing holding onto him and dragging him down tightened its grip on his ankle. He had to get to the surface, and all he could think of was to kick it. He kicked continuously as hard as he could with a booted heel, hitting his ankle a few times, but he didn't care. He knew he had to escape or be dragged down into the dark waters.

Visions of the lady in the water all those years ago resurfaced, and Torsten remembered his father's mangled corpse. He didn't want to end up like his father. With all his strength, he kicked as hard as he could one more time. The monster let go, and he was free to swim to the surface.

Once his face felt the wind, he opened his eyes and sucked in deep breaths of air, filling his lungs. Before the monster could attack him again, he swam as hard and as fast as he could until his feet felt rocks and sand.

The other men dragged themselves to shore where they collapsed onto the sand, exhausted.

Once most of Torsten's body was out of the water, he fell to his knees. The lapping of the water still touched his feet, and he doubted the monster could get him in shallow water. Finally, he relaxed and caught his breath.

Torsten's vision was no longer blurry and dark, and he could discern the shapes of the men beside me. A sharp shooting pain from his ankle caused him to fall onto his ass and survey the damage done. Pulling up his pants, it left only the woolen sock on that foot; the monster had ripped off his boot. The goatskin of his other boot had pulled apart. There had to be extra boots from someone, or he would kill the next animal he saw and use its skin. The monster had left a red welt around his ankle from its tight grip. Touching the raised skin sent a jolt of electricity up his leg and into his spine. Torsten gritted his teeth until the pain subsided.

"Get up, we need to go!" Erik yelled. "Ulf, Sten, Knud, see if we can salvage anything from our boats or anything that's floating near the shore. But don't go back into the sea. There's a giant octopus out there, and it almost got Torsten."

The men grunted and walked along the coast for something that they could still use or eat.

"Are you injured?"

Torsten shook his head.

"Good. Now come." Erik outstretched a hand to pull him up. "I saw a way out over there." He pointed to an area between rocks.

"We lost men, Erik. Shouldn't we wait for the others to swim to shore first? Or at least let us catch our breaths."

"No, come. Those who made it to shore need shelter before nightfall." Erik raised a bushy brow and scratched his red beard. "Let's find a cave or somewhere we can make a fire, and only then can we rest."

Torsten nodded and followed reluctantly with a limp, the pain manageable.

The path between two rocks was tight and steep, but, once they were through it, they stood on a cliff with the rough sea in front of them, with caves and mountains covered in snow behind them.

"Where's the village?" Torsten asked, staring at the mountain.

"That way." Erik pointed left, which meant they had to travel along the coastline and between the mountains.

Torsten slowly shook his head. They would not make it,

and he dared not voice his opinion or Erik the Red would crush his skull.

"Make a fire while I hunt for food."

Torsten pulled his axe loose from his belt and chopped fallen dead trees. They needed to dry their clothing before nightfall and gather as much firewood as possible. Snow fell continuously here, and the chill had already settled into his bones. But he had survived the raid, the monster, and the swim to shore. It was unfortunate they had lost so many men this voyage, but they would celebrate their lives once they returned to the village and see about getting more men to join them from Iceland.

The men grunted as they emerged from between the steep rocky path, carrying various supplies they had gathered.

Njal, the tallest of them, dropped a shoe before Torsten. "It's the only one I could find. Hope it fits."

"I'm not picky. Thanks," Torsten said and hit the flint with a rock and sparks lit the wood. He blew quickly and gently on it, added dry materials and watched it flare to life. The fire burned quickly, setting the wood ablaze, and he felt the warmth.

The rest of the men had joined Torsten by the time Erik yelled from where he stood, holding up the carcasses of his latest catch—at least four hares. That's just one reason he was their chieftain; he was an exceptional hunter. The other, he had brought them to Greenland to make it their home.

Erik skinned the hares and set them above the fire to cook. Their clothing was drying, the snow had stopped falling, and it wasn't as freezing. The men had found jugs of mead, coats, the treasure they had looted, and two tents for at least four to sleep comfortably.

Once the moon was above their camp, they had eaten

and had finished two jugs of mead; they settled in to get some rest. Tomorrow would be another hard day of walking the rough terrain to their village and to their women. Torsten missed Grunhild and their boy. He couldn't wait to show her how much he missed her.

Torsten's body ached so much, and, even though he was used to sleeping on the ground, tonight it proved hard and uncomfortable. When he finally slept, his dreams came in flashes—the monster drowning him, holding his ankle so tightly it severed his foot, bits of torn flesh being the only sign he had a foot. And then he died, a combination of drowning and bleeding to death in the depths of Hell.

The shrill cries of something brought him to the surface and from his dream. But the cries were not his from the dream. The cries continued somewhere behind the rock they had settled on, and, as it cried, scratching sounds started as though it was creeping up the side of the cliff.

Whatever it was, it knew they were here. They'd never seen any monster on this land before, and Torsten didn't want to wait and find out if it was friendly.

Torsten nudged Erik awake. "Erik, wake up. Do you hear that?"

"What?" Erik groaned as he sat upright, wiping sleep from his eyes.

The cries sounded again, and it changed to a deep-throated growl as if the monster sensed they had woken.

"What's that?"

"I don't know, but it's coming closer."

"Wake up," Erik said sternly to the rest of the crew.

A scream pierced the air, and Thorsten's ears throbbed; it felt as though someone was digging into his eardrum. All the men crouched and held their hands over their ears to muffle the sound. Blood oozed from under Knud's hands, with pain etched on his face. It felt as though Torsten's ears were being ripped from his head. The scratching against the rocks behind them grew louder as the monster crawled nearer.

When the screaming finally stopped, they stood like statues and stared behind them, waiting in breathless anticipation. The moon was not big or bright enough for them to see what was there, and the fire was only a few red coals with smoke.

"Pick up what you can and come this way," Erik whispered. "We need to leave now."

Knud was trying not to make a sound, even though Torsten imagined the amount of pain he must be in. The dark liquid from his ears had stopped running as he wiped it off the side of his head and neck. Torsten didn't think he could hear. Knud looked confused as he stared at everyone with his brows knitted together.

Torsten waved a hand in front of Knud's face and beckoned him over and pointed to where Erik had walked.

Knud nodded in understanding, picked up what he could and walked in front.

The other men carried the rest but left the tents. It would take too long to disassemble and pack them. If they had a chance, they could return, but Torsten wouldn't want to. He wanted to get home. Torsten carried two bags and a jug of mead and brought up the rear.

They were ten men, and, even though they could fight, they had no idea what monster crept behind them. It was not a monster they had heard of through stories around the fire. This monster sounded large and angry. Had they stumbled upon its lair? Was this its territory?

As much as Torsten wanted to understand what it was, he didn't want to wait for it. It sounded hungry.

As quietly as they could, they descended the rocks until they reached the ground. The hard, loose gravel crunched beneath their boots. The monster's roar echoed against the rocks, and Torsten's arms pebbled.

The earth shook when it jumped on the rocks behind him.

"Run!" Erik yelled.

They ran, the uneven ground dark beneath their feet. Now and then, Torsten would kick a rock that stood out below. Men tripped and fell, stood up and ran again. Others stumbled without falling. The monster's shrill cry sounded closer, and the ground shook again.

Torsten's heart pounded. His chest heaved as he ran. He squeezed the axe in his hand, ready to use it on the monster behind them. He was sure everyone felt the same as he heard grunts when men crashed to the ground, while others pulled them back up again. Torsten didn't want to look over his shoulder. He could feel the monster was behind them.

With each leap it took, the stones rose and fell to the ground, shaking the earth. The monster roared behind him, and a flash of light guided their way.

That's when Torsten turned around. He stopped running and stared up at the monstrosity.

The creature was as tall as a mountain; its mouth was wide and opened four ways—top lip, bottom lip, and lips that opened on either side. Sharp pointy teeth filled its mouth. Each time it made a sound, all the lips pulled open and a blue-orange flame sparked to life. The monster shot red fire from its mouth near their heads. The smell of burned hair wafted in the air.

Its evil eyes found Torsten. He froze. The ground shook. It neared. Torsten's pulse thundered in his ears, and a cold, numb feeling washed over him.

"Torsten, what are you doing? Run!" Erik yanked Torsten backward, caught him before he fell and forced him to turn around before the fire roasted them both.

They ran along the edge with the sound of the sea on one side and rounded a bend behind rocks. They stopped when they reached a steep cliff with a narrow ledge. Below them, the rough seas splashed against the side of the mountain.

The men maneuvered quickly along the ledge, then the monster jumped over their cliff and landed on the other side. Erik and Torsten froze. The men did not. The monster made that awful ear-piercing sound again; they crouched and covered their ears as the monster jumped onto their cliff and scooped up the men in its giant flaming mouth. Blood squirted and dribbled from between its teeth. Its tongue flicked to catch Bjorn, who had fallen. The men's cries were loud and soul piercing, then ... silence.

Erik and Torsten crouched motionless in the cliff's shadows. The monster either didn't see them or couldn't. He wasn't sure. Torsten heard his pulse hammer in his ears and marveled that he could after all the noise the monster had made; he was sure he would've been deaf.

Erik gripped his shoulder, placed his finger to his mouth. He too realized the monster couldn't see them—but it could hear them.

A combination of blue and purple scales shimmered in the soft light of the half-silver moon. It had long, sharp talons, with a tail that whipped from side to side. Its head was large to accommodate its maw that opened wide, and it boasted black orbs for eyes. Its flat nose was two holes in the middle of its face. This was not a dragon nor the Jormungandr that lived in the sea, and it wasn't the Jotnar —the giants and devourers from their stories. This monster was something else, something unknown. Something from an unfamiliar land.

It screamed that ear-shattering sound while gills on its side opened, and a red light glowed from within, as if its blood was something foreign to what Torsten knew. When it turned to face the opposite side, Torsten noticed the sharp ridges that started at the back of its head down to its tail. It leaped up and over the ledge; the earth shook as it disappeared from where it had come.

"We are berserkers and must kill that beast, Erik." Thorsten knew they needed to avenge their brothers, and what better way to go into battle than with a crew crazed as dogs or wolves and as strong as bears or bulls. With their shields and axes, they had slain men; slaying the beast would be a treat.

Erik nodded in the darkness and stood. "Yes, Torsten, we do. Let's see where it sleeps."

They walked back the way they had come until they arrived at their campsite. The beast had destroyed their tents, and the fire was nothing but a fine smoke. Orange and yellow light cast against the sky as the sun rose, providing them with light. They peered over the ledge from where the monster had come; it was a straight drop into darkness. A shudder ran through Torsten. To reach the monster, they had to go into the abyss. They were putting their lives at risk, and it would be their honor to do so.

Without saying a word, they knew what they had to do. Erik climbed down on the right and Torsten on the left, and they descended into the darkness of the unknown.

For a while, Torsten could still see Erik, but the deeper he descended into the thick darkness, the less he could see him.

A low rumble was audible. The monster's slow and

steady breathing indicated it was inside and resting. The floor was comprised of old ribcages, splintered bones, and skulls.

Torsten carefully stepped on the bones, and they crunched beneath his boots. The sound echoed within the cave; he stopped and listened, but the crunching continued. Erik too was heading in the rumbling sound's direction.

Once Torsten's eyes had adjusted to the darkness, he saw movement—the steady outline of the beast's body moving up and down as it breathed. He followed against the side of the cave until he was so close to the monster he could touch it, but he didn't want to. Not yet.

Being in a confined space with something that could easily kill him was not the best tactical advantage. Even though he held his axe, he couldn't kill it from this angle. Perhaps if he was beneath it and hacked at its neck. Torsten also didn't know if it had a heart, and, if it did, where did it sit inside its body? Its skin could be thick and impossible to penetrate.

This wasn't the best time to wonder what to do with a monster so big and deadly, but he was here, and so was Erik.

Torsten stepped backward, and a bone splintered. The sound was loud enough to wake anything. He sucked in his breath and held it. He didn't move.

An eye opened, and two pupils surrounded by two irises in that one orb focused on him. It grunted, and a red light glowed from its gills on the side of its head.

Erik screamed on the other side of the beast and ran toward the monster.

It moved its head away from Torsten and slowly rose. Plumes of smoke emitted from its tiny nostrils as it readied itself to blast fire from its mouth.

Torsten screamed and ran under its body with his axe high in the air. As hard as he could, he sliced into its neck, and, as it started rising, Torsten's axe tore through its chest to its belly. Dark liquid oozed from the widening wound and rained on him. The dark ichor went into his eyes, ears, over his body, and, as much as he didn't want to, he swallowed the metal and coal-flavored blood. Torsten gagged and spit what he could, but he had already swallowed so much of it.

The monster bellowed that ear-piercing sound and lunged forward.

Torsten jumped out of its way before it crushed him.

It jerked forward one last time and crumpled to the floor. Black blood spilled across the ground and covered him again.

The silence was loud in the cave. There were no other sounds other than Torsten's deep-chested breathing.

"Erik?" Torsten finally yelled as panic rose within him. "Erik!"

"Yeah," Erik replied hoarsely.

"You okay?"

"It caught me." He grunted in pain.

Torsten rose to his feet. Now that he was empty-handed after burying his axe inside the monster, he wasn't sure whether it was dead, so he walked carefully around it, giving it a wide girth.

The blue and purple scales no longer shined. The red gills on its side were dark. There was no smoke. Even though its eyes were open, it was not seeing.

Torsten was so close to its face he could see the monster; two white pupils surrounded by two clear blue irises sat inside each dark orb. Tiny blue and purple scales covered its face like feathers, and, even though it looked soft and delicate, it was not. If it wasn't so scary or hungry, it could've been beautiful. Its mouth that opened wide on four sides was closed and unmoving.

A shudder ran through Torsten. He'd been close to death so many times he'd lost count, but this event was an everlasting memory.

"Torsten?"

"Yes, brother. I'm coming." Torsten raced around the beast's head and away from its sharp claws that stretched in front of its body. He froze when he saw Erik, who was underneath the monster's claw, his abdomen sliced in half by a talon but not all the way through. His guts had spilled out, and his ribs glistened in the bleak light.

Erik coughed; his red blood mixed with the black ichor that was now surrounding them. "Look after the village, brother. Keep everyone safe." Red spittle fell on his chin. He closed his eyes and took his last breath.

Even though they had killed the monster, they had lost everyone. Torsten knew he needed to return to the village and celebrate the lives of the men who had sacrificed everything. It would be the best ceremony to ensure all their men a safe trip to Valhalla.

He tried to wipe the blood off his face, but all he did was smudge it from side to side; he needed to clean properly and find a way out of this cave without having to climb the rock face again.

Exhaustion engulfed Torsten, but the need to return to the village was greater. He walked over the skeletons of thousands of men toward the entrance when a light on the right caught his eye.

Walking toward it, he saw it was a treasure of gold, rubies, and diamonds stashed here by the monster or by the men who thought they were safe in the cave. Torsten didn't care which and grabbed handfuls of the precious items and stuffed his pockets. He found an old bag and filled that too. The village would welcome this treasure as compensation for the women who had lost husbands. When satisfied he had enough, a wind caressed his face; he headed in that direction through a narrow tunnel toward an exit which opened to a beautiful land—an oasis on snow-covered land adorned with flowers of all colors, shapes, and sizes and a waterfall of stunning cerulean water in which to drink and clean.

Once he'd quenched his thirst and washed, with heavy pockets, he walked through the bushes, flowers, and trees. He walked hungry and exhausted and didn't stop until the familiar sounds of children playing and women singing told him he was home. The last thing he remembered hearing was screaming and Grunhild cradling his head in her lap.

When he woke, he was in fresh clothing and in his bed. His head throbbed with one of the worst aches he'd ever experienced. Placing his hand to his forehead, he was feverish too.

"You're awake," his wife's familiar voice said.

Relieved to know he was home and not in that cave or being chased by the monster, Torsten turned his head slowly toward her and smiled.

"I'm so glad you're home. How are you feeling?"

"Better now that I'm safe."

She wore an expression he hadn't seen often—serious and full of concern. "What happened, Torsten? Where are the other men? And where did you get all the treasure from?"

"It was a beast so big and deadly. It killed the men with one lick of its tongue. Then Erik and I found its lair and killed it."

"Where is Erik?"

He shook his head. He couldn't bring himself to say it.

"No ..." Inga sobbed.

Torsten hadn't known she was in the room until she spoke.

"I'm sorry, Inga. I truly am. I tried my best to stop the beast from going after Erik. It was too big and hungry for death." He swallowed hard. Pain ripped through his abdomen like a claw tearing through his flesh. He grunted in pain, clutching his stomach.

"Are you all right?" Grunhild asked as she came to his aid. "Your stomach?" She lifted off his hands and pulled down the fur blanket. She gasped.

He glanced down. His stomach was turning shades of purple and blue with a light silver shine.

"What happened to you that caused you to bruise this badly?"

It reminded Torsten of how the monster's scales had shone in the light. Was it only bruising? He didn't want to cause anyone to panic, certainly not Grunhild or their son. "I'll be fine. It's only bruising from the fight with the monster." He sat upright. "Where is the treasure now?"

"With the elders." She glanced at Inga.

"What is it?" Torsten stared from Inga to Grunhild. "What aren't you telling me?"

"The elders ... They are concerned."

"About what? That the monster will return?"

Both women nodded.

"We killed the monster. Sliced it from throat to belly. It won't be returning. I give you my word." Torsten threw off the fur blanket and sat on the edge of the bed. "Help me up."

Grunhild came to his aid again, wrapping an arm around his waist, and helped him stand.

When he was certain he wouldn't fall, he waved her away. "Let me dress, so I can speak with everyone."

Grunhild stayed behind to help, but he told her to leave him alone.

Before pulling on a shirt, Torsten stared at the bruises that had now spread to his chest, the blue and purple colors prominent. Something was protruding under his left nipple. It was hard, like a fingernail. At first, he flicked it to see if it would come loose, but it didn't. That one flick only caused a sharp shooting pain that shocked his chest and moved into his back, as if whatever it was had been connected to the nerves running along his spine. His skin ran icy as heat ran through his body. He had to get it out.

He grasped it between his fingertips and yanked. The object came out, but the pain rocked him backward, and he fell onto the bed as blood poured out the fresh wound. His mouth fell open as he stared at the item.

A scale.

He moved it left then right, and the light caught it, making it shine purple and blue, like the monster's scales.

Flinching as if it burned him, he threw the scale to the floor, rose to his feet and shook his head in disbelief. *This is impossible.* For a moment, all he could do was stand and stare at the scale on the floor. He was numb. Thoughts raced with reasons why this had happened and how.

Then his feet felt hot, as if he had run over hot coals. Even his body felt fiery, as though he was running a temperature, even though he felt fine. Or he was shocked because of the scale he'd just pulled from his chest and relieved his body wasn't hurting anymore.

His legs buckled, and he crashed to the ground. On his hands and knees, the heat coursed through his hips and up his spine. When it reached his head, he screamed. That ear-piercing sound he'd heard before was coming out of *his* mouth.

Torsten's back rounded, and he hung his head low as popping sounds emanated from his spine. One, two, three, four … until he'd counted ten. He felt his spine with his right hand, and his fingers caressed rough bonelike spikes protruding through his skin. The heat he had felt earlier disappeared like a wave leaving shore and was replaced with ice. If he was changing into something sinister, he had to leave the village before he hurt someone. Torsten knew he had to leave his family before they discovered what he'd become—the monster he had killed.

Was it the treasure he had taken from the cave or the black blood he had reluctantly swallowed that was the catalyst of his demise?

The cold washed away, leaving fire in its wake; it wasn't heat, it was pure fire.

He climbed to his feet and ran out the room and out the house.

Grunhild called after him, but Torsten couldn't hear what she was saying; the sounds of his beating heart filled his ears, and all he could do not to kill her was to run.

Grey clouds gathered. The wind had changed direction and blasted leaves around him. Thunder roared as lightning flashed.

The pure fire receded within him and was replaced with thirst and hunger. Torsten wanted to eat Grunhild and every villager. He wanted to drink their blood, chew on their meat and lick their bones.

Torsten knew he had to get away before his desire for flesh overrode his common sense not to hurt anyone he cared for. He ran until he was on the outskirts of the village. Lightning blazed across the sky as the grey clouds grew darker and angrier. When the thunder rumbled, it felt as though the weather storm was aimed at Torsten, that the gods were unhappy with what he had done and showed their dissatisfaction.

Torsten ran so fast he tripped and crashed to the ground. Glancing over his shoulder, he saw Grunhild standing in the doorjamb of their house, calling after him. But it was no use; he couldn't go back. He was changing, and nothing could stop it.

Pain tore through his chest. He roared as his body was pulled backward; his bones broke and skin split. The beast ripped through his flesh like one would remove a shirt and discard it on the ground.

When it was quiet and the earth was still, Torsten opened his eyes. He saw what the monster saw—the world below his claws, the scales for skin that shone purple and blue in a cave he now called home.

And the only thing on his mind, he was *ravenous*.

TWO

The Holiday

MARTY
Mexico, Circa 2012

Marty wrapped his meaty arm around Stacey and pulled her closer to his body. He was harder now that she was so close to him and relieved nobody could see his frontside.

She squealed with excitement and oblivious to the fact she excited him. "We're finally on holiday, hun." She pressed her chin against his chest and stared up at him, pouting. "Are you thinking about work?"

"No. We have a week all to ourselves, and, for once, I won't be thinking about anything except you and this place. It's all you, babe." He leaned in for a kiss, and she squealed. "Just stop with the loud noises. I don't think my ears can handle any more."

She playfully slapped his chest.

"Come, I want to set up camp before the sun sets." Marty took her hand to traverse the path many hikers have used before them.

La Cañada was one of the regular tourist destinations with plenty of hotels, but he wanted an authentic holiday with nature and everything in between. Marty wanted them to take their time exploring the various Mayan temples and stay in the best camping spots off the beaten track. He'd had enough of buildings, cellphones, and people. The past year, he had done nothing but work during the week till late in the evenings and even on most weekends. He had promised Stacey months ago they would go on vacation, but he always had to push it out, and the look of devastation in her eyes made his chest ache; he hated seeing her unhappy. Then, last week, his boss had told him he could go and insisted on two weeks; they would spend one week here and one week at home—he wanted to do a few things around the house.

A bus took tourists straight to the various temples, but Marty wanted to hike from the one to the other. As a child, his family went on vacations in any forest his parents wanted to visit and all over the world; money was never an object. Nature was in his blood, and sitting in a bus and taken to their destination was cheating in his eyes.

Their first day, they ambled the short distance to the Temple of the Cross and Temple of the Inscriptions from the nearby town. When they arrived, they strolled up and around the temples, admiring their architecture, brilliance, and structure. They had cordoned off some areas from tourists, but pictures were allowed.

Marty and Stacey went at a time of year where there were enough tourists to fill five busses, and it elated Marty they were hiking everywhere.

Marty walked around the people and stood a few steps from them while regarding the temples. Stacey didn't mind the crowds and pushed through to take better pictures.

Marty glanced at his phone and pulled Stacey's free hand.

She was jotting down features of the temple in her journal; she'd told him she wanted to remember this holiday forever and one day tell their kids about it. When he pulled her hand, the pen left a lengthy line down the page. She huffed in displeasure of her ruined page and the interruption.

"If we want to get to the waterfalls by nightfall, we have to leave now." He continued walking while maintaining an iron grip on her hand.

"You made me ruin this page." She held up her journal to show him.

He shrugged.

"Did you at least see anything, or were you too busy looking at your phone?" Her tone was clipped and dripping with sarcasm.

He stopped and waited for her to stand in front of him. "The only reason I look at my phone is to see the time, Stacey."

She looked everywhere but at him.

"Look at me." His voice was loud enough that other people stopped to glance at them but quickly continued with their sightseeing to avoid the impending fight.

Stacey raised her head but averted her eyes. She couldn't look at the people surrounding them either.

Marty rubbed her cheek with a calloused thumb from weight training.

Her skin reddened beneath his rough hands.

He arched an eyebrow, grabbed her chin, raised it until her eyes met his and waited for her apology.

"Sorry. I didn't mean it," she said softly, barely a whisper. Her blue eyes sparkled with moisture.

"Good girl." Marty pulled her closer and kissed her forehead. "Are you ready now?" he asked gently then draped an arm around her shoulders. He fixed his backpack, so it was straighter, and helped Stacey with hers.

"Yes, let's get to the waterfall. I've seen the beautiful pictures online. Now I want to see it for real." She beamed up at him, which made him happy, and he forgot her brief outburst.

They left the temples and headed toward the Agua Azul Waterfalls. They followed the path of those before them, resting twice before pushing ahead, only snacking on a protein bar each during their hike.

They arrived at the turquoise water pools as the sun set. Because they had reached the waterfall from the top and not the bottom, they didn't have to go through the tiny village or pay the sixty pesos entrance fee. From where they stood, they saw the village on the left-hand side with a market where the locals sold trinkets that kept their little village thriving. In the village, they offered bed and breakfasts, cafes, and restaurants, but none made it on the one-star list.

Stacey exhaled audibly, dropped her backpack to the ground, kicked off her shoes and fell into the water. "Come join me," she called out before plunging into the blue water again.

Marty gently set his backpack on the grass beside Stacey's, removed his shirt, folded it, placed it on top of his backpack then removed his socks and shoes. He jumped into the water, splashing Stacey as she came up for air. They laughed as they swam in the cool, refreshing water. For a moment, they forgot about the world they were in.

Marty pulled Stacey against him.

She wrapped her legs around his waist and her arms around his neck, and they kissed.

Twigs snapped behind them. Marty spun them around and saw a boy about thirteen with olive skin and black hair. His brown eyes were wide, his mouth parted. What caught Marty's attention was the knife in the boy's hand.

"Hey?" Stacey said with a quiver in her voice. She too had noticed the teenager was armed.

The boy yelled something in Spanish and ran back from where he had come.

"Are you sure we're allowed to be up here?" Stacey asked with that same nervousness.

"Of course."

"When you were here with your brother, did you come this side too?"

"Uh-huh." He let go of her, waded toward the edge of the pool and climbed out. "I think he's gone. Did the knife look clean to you? I'm sure I saw blood on it."

"It looked clean to me." Stacey climbed out and stood beside him. "Let's move away from here and find a spot to have dinner. I'm hungry for real food."

"You're always hungry." He walked around the edge and collected his clothing.

Once dressed, they walked farther up the hill and through dense leafy trees. When they found a descent high-rise spot where they were well hidden, they set up camp.

Their three-man dome tent was constructed, with their backpacks inside. They didn't want to make a fire and alert anyone to their site, so they warmed their potatoes and chicken over a portable stove. They ate in silence while admiring the sea of stars above them and the moving lights of the tiny village below.

"Do you think the boy will come back to look for us?"

Stacey broke the silence with a question that had been swarming inside Marty's head since he saw the boy.

"No. I don't think so. He may have been fishing, and we caught him off guard." He hoped that was the situation and didn't want to raise alarms and cause Stacey to panic. It was their first night, and he didn't want to ruin it so soon with speculation of an armed boy. Who knew what the boy wanted? Marty cursed himself silently for learning French instead of Spanish.

They finished their meal in silence and watched the full blood moon drift across the sky. It felt peaceful yet strange. Being out here without hardly any lights to drown out the stars, he could see the moon, although its color was remarkably eerie.

They cleaned the cutlery and readied for bed. It was late, and he wanted to get an early start and head for the next temple in Tonina, which was a sixteen-hour hike.

The next morning, they woke as the sun rose, shining golden drops on their skin through the tiny holes in their tent. Stacey inserted a fresh pair of contacts that only lasted twenty-four hours. They dressed and packed their things.

Stacey frantically searched for something, walking to one side of their camp then the other.

"What are you looking for?" Marty asked as he pulled on his backpack.

"Our portable stove. I'm positive I left it outside near our cutlery last night. This morning, it's gone."

A chill ran through Marty as he recalled the teenager with the knife. He could have possibly taken their stove. Marty would have to look out for him in case he followed them.

"No matter. We have to go," Marty blurted as calmly as he could for Stacey's sake and started walking. "We need to get a move on if we want to reach our next camp site by nightfall."

Stacey wanted to say something, but she bit her lip and followed.

They walked, and occasionally, Marty would glance behind them to ensure they were still alone. If the teenager was the one who had taken their portable stove, it was possible he had stolen it so he could sell it to unsuspecting tourists and make a quick dollar. He couldn't blame the boy, but it was inconvenient for them.

He and Stacey rested every hour and absorbed their scenery, often stopping when they came to an area where they could sit and admire the breathtaking views.

Even though Marty continued checking whether someone was following them, he didn't see anyone, but he felt *something*. It was a strange sensation, like ants walking over his skin or a snail slithering up his leg. He felt something around them; he just couldn't see it.

He grabbed his side and felt the hardness of the handle, and lower was the sheath. It was the only self-defense weapon he preferred and was skilled at using. He'd been to the shooting range but hated the ease in which a bullet could kill. He favored the up-close and personal dance of a knife fight. After their encounter with the boy, he'd decided to keep it on his belt, just in case.

The sun set, and the trees bathed them in shadowy darkness. They each switched on their flashlight to see their way.

Marty checked his compass, ensuring they were still on the right path. When he saw the lights that surrounded the temple, they made camp a short distance away, so they could be the first ones to inspect the structure at daybreak.

He set up the tent while Stacey prepared their vegetable

wraps for dinner. All day, they had snacked on nuts, protein bars, and water; they craved warm food.

They settled down and ate.

The evening was quiet. All Marty heard was their chewing; he stopped and listened.

"What's wrong?" Stacey asked with a mouth full of food.

"Finish what's in your mouth before speaking. It's gross." He listened again. "Do you hear that?"

She shrugged.

"It's too quiet. There's nothing. No birds, not even insects. It's dead quiet here."

"Hmm," Stacey added while she ate.

"Never mind." Perhaps it was only Marty who felt out of sorts. It had been a while since he'd been on vacation. He must've been more tired than he'd thought.

They finished their wraps and sat for a while. Exhausted from their hike, they decided to sleep early. Once they settled in their tent, Stacey removed her contacts, and they removed their shoes. They couldn't be bothered with washing; they would do that when it was daylight and they could see where they were. They slipped into their sleeping bag, and Marty pulled Stacey into him and fell asleep immediately.

———

Marty walked around the waterfall, admiring the blue water. Something moved below the surface heading toward him. He crouched to see what it was. The boy jumped from the water with outstretched arms and a knife in one hand. Screams pierced his dream, and Marty jackknifed from their shared sleeping bag.

"Stacey?" he called out when she wasn't beside him. Trying to catch his breath from his nightmare, Marty only felt worse thinking something had happened to Stacey. He pictured her bleeding somewhere he couldn't see. He zipped open the tent and climbed out. "Stacey?"

"It's okay. I'm over here," she answered from a distance, sounding dreamlike, as if she were in the trees.

"Where are you?" Marty walked in the direction he thought she had called from.

"I'm here," she said from behind him.

He flinched when she spoke. "Jesus, you gave me a fright. What were you doing?" He neared but stopped when he noticed something dark on her shirt. "What's this?"

"Huh?" She glanced down. "Oh, I was using the bathroom when I scared myself." She chuckled. "I must've dirtied my fingers then touched my shirt." She rubbed her shirt, smudging it.

"Is it mud?"

"It must be. The sand was very soft." She giggled and swayed, losing balance, but Marty caught her before she fell.

"Are you drunk?"

"*Noo* ..." she drawled.

"Sorry. That was us," a man said and approached them. "We meant no harm."

A woman came out from behind him. "We were camping not too far away from you and smoking." She smiled sinisterly, her dark eyes shining silver in the moonlight. She raised her hand to reveal a joint. "I think our smoke got to her."

Stacey burst out laughing then collapsed.

"She can't even drink. You can only imagine what that stuff does to her." Marty picked her up and headed for their tent. Once she was in and sound asleep, he returned to their uninvited guests. "Where are you from?"

"All over really. We're travel bloggers," the woman said, pulled on the joint and handed it to the man. "I'm Kerry. That's Luke." She offered her hand.

Marty stared at her bony fingers, but Kerry wasn't about to pull back her hand until he shook it. Eventually, he did, and Luke's.

"You want some?" Luke offered their joint to him, his smile broad and venomous. In the moonlight, their pale skin held a shine to it like plastic or spandex.

Marty blinked, trying to make sense of what he was seeing, but their skin seemed normal. He was only tired. "No thanks. Where is your camp?" He looked around but didn't see where they could be.

"Through those trees." Luke pointed to the side. "We endured a long hike here, and we smoke to relax. You sure you don't want?"

"No. I'm good." Marty's tone was clipped as he waved the smoke from his face. When he saw their expression change, tightening of their lips and lines between their eyes, he decided he didn't want to upset people he'd just met. "Thanks anyway. I'm not much of a smoker."

"No problem." Luke shrugged. "Anyway, are you guys going to the temple in the morning?"

As much as Marty wanted to say no, it was obvious they were here for the temple. There was no point lying. He didn't know what the couple was capable of and decided to tell the truth. "Yes. And you?"

"That's why we're here. Perhaps we'll see you for breakfast, and we can check it out together."

Marty cringed, but, instead of saying what he truly felt,

he said, "Sure," and bit his tongue to say anything more. Even though his words were bitter, he would swallow them.

"It's settled then." Luke slapped Marty's back, sending a jolt of lightning through his body that made him stand taller. "See you at sunrise."

Marty groaned as he zipped up his tent, shaking his head at the words he didn't say to get them out of the situation with the new couple. He did not like them; they looked weird, smelled like weed, and who knew what else they were up to. They better not be swingers, or he would use his knife on them to protect himself and Stacey.

He glanced at his girl. She seemed peaceful and angelic. He leaned in for a kiss on her cheek, and she moved her arm over his stomach. Marty settled in for one of the deepest and darkest sleeps he had ever had.

When they woke the next morning, Marty stretched. His muscles weren't cramping, and his feet weren't aching. His eyes felt wider, and the colors of the world around them seemed clearer and brighter. He wondered if it was the aftereffect of the strain of weed Luke and Kerry had smoked near them. He could only imagine what it did to them if he felt so good.

When Stacey woke, she yawned and stretched then climbed out the tent on all fours. When she stood, she had the widest smile he had ever seen.

"You look like you just got laid," Marty teased.

"Oh man. I don't know what that couple smoked, but whatever strain it's made of, I feel good this morning." She squinted. "I don't have to put in my contacts." A chortle escaped her lips. "How weird is that, Marty? I can see without my contacts." She put on the pair of glasses she kept in case her contacts irritated her eyes and shook her head. "Nope. It's blurry with them on. Well …" She shrugged. "I'm not complaining.

"Good morning, gentle folk," Luke said as he entered their camp sight. "Are you ready?"

"We just woke up and haven't eaten yet." Marty pulled a trail mix from his backpack. "I would prefer powdered eggs, but we lost our portable stove."

"You're welcome to use ours." Kerry retrieved it from her backpack and handed it to Stacey.

"Huh, looks just like the one we had," she said and pulled the packet of powdered eggs from her bag.

"We only have enough for us, but, if you want, I'm sure I can share it," Stacey offered.

"No, thank you," Kerry said. "We've already eaten." Her smile seemed tight and barely curved at the edges.

Stacey and Marty ate quickly while Luke and Kerry watched them. Their expressions were unreadable. They finished, packed up their tent and followed the other couple to the temple.

Only a handful of tourists were taking pictures of the temple, which meant Marty had the space to survey the temple without someone bumping into him. He noted the intricate detail of the carvings on the stone the Mayans had made and reached to touch it. Before he could feel what they had felt all those years ago, Stacey pulled his arm, jumping up and down with excitement.

"What is it? You're like a schoolgirl."

"Oh hush. Nothing's wrong with a little ecstasy." She hugged him then pulled away. "Listen, Kerry was telling me they found a secret way inside." Her gaze flitted to the side where the other couple stood, staring at them.

"Are you nuts? I'm not going into an unknown tight

enclosure with people we don't know. They could be murderers."

She offered him her deadpan face. "Really? Is that what you think of them? They're cool, Marty. *Pleeeaze*. I want to go."

He shook his head. "No. I'm sorry, but no. They give me a terrible feeling when I'm near them."

"Really? Hun, there's nothing to worry about. What can they do to us? The temple isn't that big anyway. We'll be in and out of it in an hour, maximum."

He sighed reluctantly. "I don't like it. I really don't."

"Hey, guys. Are you ready? It's a small temple, so we should be about thirty minutes. The door opens up here, and I doubt this one goes very deep." Luke's smile reached his eyes.

"Have you been inside before?"

"No. It was by chance we discovered it. Kerry went inside a way and didn't want to continue without me. I wanted to offer you the chance to join us. Or you can stay here and wait for us. Then we tell you how it was."

"I want to go." Stacey gave Marty her puppy-dog eyes and pouted. "Pretty please."

Marty felt his sheathed knife and exhaled. "Okay fine, but stay with me. We don't know what's inside."

Stacey bounced all the way to the temple's secret entrance.

Once they moved the block of stone to the side, it had revealed a narrow passage. Luke entered first with Kerry holding onto his hand, then Stacey with Marty bringing up the rear. He held onto Stacey's hand like a vise grip. The deeper they walked, the darker the narrow passage became and the lighter the air.

Beads of sweat dripped from Marty's face, and his

clothing stuck to his body. His backpack felt heavier the farther they traversed. Marty glanced over his shoulder and noticed a black hole had swallowed the sunlight, and he wondered how far they had walked and if they had maneuvered around corners that blocked his vision of the entrance. "Hey, guys. How far do you think we've walked?"

"Not sure, but we should come up the other side soon. It's not a big temple," Luke offered.

The walls seemed to close in on them. Marty saw less and less of the other couple as they walked faster, and he and Stacey walked slower. Finally, they disappeared; it was only the two of them.

"Hey, guys? Where are you?" Stacey asked with a quiver, fighting back tears. "Marty, I'm scared." She stopped walking and reached for him.

He saw the outline of her body in the thick blackness and that was all. The walls touched his shoulders on either side as he held onto Stacey. He was grateful his backpack didn't get him stuck.

"Let's go back." He turned but held onto Stacey's arms while she clung to him.

She wrapped her arms around his waist, and they walked the way they had come.

Marty heard Stacey whimper behind him. He suddenly felt panic now that they were alone and in a suffocating tunnel. He tried to push it aside, but he was failing. His heart hammered as he tried to feel his way out. The walls were damp beneath his fingertips, and the air became warmer and heavier. He struggled to breathe; the more air he sucked in, the less air came out.

When his head connected with a wall, he felt the hot thick liquid drip down his face. "How the hell did a wall get here? We didn't take any other paths to get here." His loud voice echoed in the hollow passage.

"What's happening, Marty?" She didn't let go of him even while he was bleeding and tried to turn around and away from the dead end.

The backpack hooked on the stone wall, and the tightness he had felt earlier had returned. "We have to go back." He pried Stacey's arms from him, so he could try to stop the head wound from bleeding. "Just give me a second, Stace. I need to stop the bleeding."

"No, no, no. Please don't let go of me."

"Here, hold on to my hips. I need to tear my shirt and stop the bleeding." He ripped the bottom of his shirt and pressed it to his head. They had forgotten their first aid kit at home, and this would have to do. "Turn around a little, so we can try to find a way out of here."

"Okay," she whispered. Her whimpering continued as she took one slow step at a time.

As quickly as they had hit the dead end, one side of the wall fell away, revealing a group of people in hooded cloaks under dim torches. The moment Marty and Stacey saw them, the crowd turned as one and glared at them through glassy eyes.

Marty and Stacey backtracked into a wall and found themselves in a corner with nowhere to go but forward, near the crowd.

There were men and women of all shapes and sizes, from what he could tell. The soft light radiating off the alcove walls was romantic and cast their faces in a sunlit hue. They raised their arms in unison and pulled on their faces. Gripping from their eyes, they pulled and stretched their skin from their heads and peeled off the outer layer. Beneath their masks revealed shiny and shimmering ebony heads. Their outer shell moved like a million worms slithering one over the other, then their skin moved outward as tentacles released from their faces. When each uncurled, it revealed a strange plastic-like slimy surface with black orbs for eyes and enormous mouths with sharp teeth.

Marty sucked in a breath and willed himself to disappear.

Stacey screamed as loud as she could until she was breathless. Her whimpering turned into a sob as they watched in horror their ultimate demise.

Deep down, Marty knew these strange creatures were about to eat them. There would be no other reason for them to be here but to satisfy their hunger.

Black mist blew past them, and he shuddered. He gripped Stacey and pulled her in front of him, clinging onto her. He tried to steady her crying, but she was most likely in shock. She would never come back from *this*. He knew he would never be the same if they ever made it out. With one free hand, he unsheathed his knife.

Screams pierced the dark wind as Kerry and Luke were brought in, bound to a totem pole with engravings that resembled Mayan carvings yet different. Who or what these creatures were, they were not Mayan—possibly the reason why they had disappeared in the first place?

The creatures chanted in foreign sounds—not a song, not a language; just a continuous thrumming of sounds and noise that neither hurt nor healed. Yet blood dripped from the tourists' ears as it forced them to listen.

They pushed Kerry and Luke into the center of the alcove where the floor moved into the walls, revealing a gaping hole.

Not realizing creatures were on either side of them, Marty only noted they were there when they touched him, and Stacey was gone. Frantically, he searched for her and called out her name. He could defend himself and get them out, but, when he reached for the knife, that too had disappeared. A cold layer of sweat covered his body even though the alcove was hot.

The creature's cold tentaclelike arms stuck to Marty's forearms, and a chill ran through his body as the slime from their tendrils seeped into him, burning his skin. The smell of burnt flesh and hair assaulted his nose, but he didn't feel pain. He only felt ... nothingness. They were numbing him was all he could think. He glanced at his arms; the slime traveled up his arms, covering him in a cool gel-like liquid while the smell of his body burning intensified.

When he could focus again, he saw Stacey between two of her own creatures. She stared at them in what he could only decipher as wonder and pure terror. He pulled on his restraints, and the tentacle's suction sucked harder. Ice-cold pain seeped into his veins and travelled throughout his nervous system, and, when it found his heart, he shuddered. It was no use. The more he tried to free himself, the more violent their grip became.

He succumbed to their will and allowed them to tie him and Stacey to their own totem pole with carvings. He couldn't recall seeing the creatures throw Luke and Kerry into the hole. He glanced over his shoulder and the enormous hole beneath them glowed lava red, orange, and yellow. The heat was suffocating, and he sucked in short shallow breaths.

"I love you, Stacey. You're my world, and I'll always treasure you."

Her whimpering continued. Between each cry, she mumbled she loved him too.

The squid creatures pushed the pole Marty and Stacey

were tied to toward the edge of the abyss and stepped back in a crescent, their inky cloaks moving in the angry wind.

The fiery light from below blasted above them like bubbles of scorching air, hitting them in their faces. Something growled, and the earth shuddered. It hissed, and sparks of ash and soot blew past them.

"Love you," was the last words to escape Marty's lips.

The monster emerged from the depths of the earth. It rose and leveled with them, and all Marty saw was the monster's gigantic head with two horns. Fire swirled in circles for eyes; its mouth slithered with licks of flames. Glancing down, Marty saw the creature was an inferno of lava. Where it had creases, a bend in the elbow, or lines in its face, lava oozed in scorching rivers of fire and coals, ready to destroy everything in its path—a demon made of lava only Hell itself could've conjured.

As the pole tilted toward the lava demon, from the corner of Marty's eye, he saw movement. He looked in that direction and saw Luke and Kerry zip their skin suit and pull on their backpacks, donning those same sinister smiles.

Then Kerry paged through Stacey's journal and winked at Marty. They were ready to bring another offering.

THREE

Keeper

BEN & STELLA
Northern Scotland, Circa 1981

Ben white-knuckled the armrest when Preston Downie, his new manager, offered him the new position. It was an exciting opportunity but also scared him. Thinking about his family moving there with him should've left him happy, but it didn't. His stomach dropped to his worn-out shoes as he crossed one foot over the other. He steadied his breathing as he exhaled a shaky breath.

"It's an immense responsibility, Ben. Are you sure you're up for the challenge?" Preston repeated the question.

Ben nodded. "Absolutely," he said confidently with a pang of guilt. His father was the fisherman, not he. Even though he had said he still fished, it had been years since he had held a rod.

"Do you understand what's required?" Again, Preston repeated the question.

Ben nodded.

"This is what the villagers have requested. You use the boat that's already there to fish. When you've caught enough, drop it off where they instruct you and go."

"Yes, sir."

"Your primary function is the lighthouse. Ensure the light works, and paint—you know, general handiwork. The only reason I'm allowing your family to join you is because everybody else had to leave the isle. I need your wife to clean their houses, so, when everyone is healthy, they can return to their homes without worrying about cleaning and all that other domestic stuff."

"Yes, sir. Agnes is grateful for the opportunity."

"Good. It makes me happy I could pay you and Agnes. Those higher up want this sorted quickly. The two of you have six months. Can I count on you?"

"Yes, sir." Ben nodded diligently again, his hands aching. He eased the vise grip he had on the armrests and rubbed his hands together, massaging one then the other.

"Right." Preston stood and offered his outstretched hand, which Ben shook. "Be at the ferry terminal at noon tomorrow. It'll only be you and your family, so there'll be space for your car. Do not be late. You know how the weather can change, and, if you're late and the weather changes, you'll be stuck on the mainland. Onboard the ferry is enough food to last a year. And you're welcomed to keep some fish you catch for yourselves."

"Thank you, sir."

"That is all." Preston dismissed Ben with a flick of the wrist.

"One question, sir."

"What is it?"

"Why?"

"Why, what?"

"Why the fish?"

"Do not concern yourself with it. Our company only provides the service to the villagers; we do not prescribe to them. Just do what I'm paying you for. And close the door on your way out." Preston sat and flipped through pages in a book, looking busy without doing actual work.

Ben closed the door as requested and exited the building. He climbed into his cream Datsun, started the little engine and drove onto the empty street. It was late afternoon and most people on the mainland were already home apart from the last few workers on the road. The chill in the air either meant a storm was brewing or passing them. With no weather reports of a storm, it had to be passing.

Ben leaned over the steering wheel and eyed the clouds. The dark cumulonimbus was low and moving fast. He drove slowly on the winding road to the little house they were renting.

Preston had offered him the principal lightkeeper position of the isle's northern lighthouse. It was something he had always wanted to do. But, to catch fish, he wasn't looking forward to that part of the job—but he would; he had to. He used to fish with his father, who had owned a fishing company. But, when his father had broken his back, he had to sell the company to pay for medical bills and keep the family going. Ben vowed not to follow in his father's footsteps and hadn't fished since.

Until now.

Ben parked on the street and turned off the ignition. He sat in darkness and watched the house where his wife and two kids resided. Agnes hadn't closed any of the curtains yet, and he saw her move across the living room to the kitchen and back. Dinner was ready, and they were waiting for him to get home.

As he watched his family move about, he thought of the other job requirement—the village handyman. He was to fix what broke while Agnes cleaned the homes. Now all he had to do was tell Agnes she would be working too.

And the reason why Agnes needed to clean the houses was the villagers had held a monthly get-together where they all brought a dish to share. The entire village had contracted food poisoning, with one death. After an investigation, they had discovered someone had cooked contaminated fish. Some thought it was an accident, others not. But everyone had become ill and went off the isle to recover in a mainland hospital.

Ben mustered the courage and entered their home. It was warmer inside than outside, with shepherd's pie assaulting his nose which made his mouth salivate.

"Mommy! Daddy's home," Harris yelled as he ran to his dad, wrapped his arms around his waist and hugged tightly. "Look here, Dad. I finally finished my model car." Harris was a builder and collector. For Christmas, they had bought him a model car kit he could assemble himself, and it took him months to put it together perfectly.

Ben bent down and surveyed the car. "Wonderful, Harris. It's perfect." He smiled at the fine job. "I couldn't have done it better myself." He ruffled Harris's hair.

"Daddy!" Stella leapt into her father's arms. The doll she held hit Ben in the face when he picked her up. A frightened expression crossed her face when she realized she had hit him with it. "Sorry, Daddy." Her bottom lip trembled.

"It's okay, sweetheart. Today is a good day." He smiled, kissed Stella on the cheek and set her down.

Agnes smiled at them, threw her dishcloth on the dining table and embraced Ben. "You got the job?"

"I got the job, and you got a job."

"Me? Why me? What do I have to do?" The lines above her eyes crinkled in the way he loved.

"For the next six months, we both have jobs that would keep us afloat for a year. And, depending on how everything goes and when the villagers return, they might extend our positions till the end of the year or indefinitely." He cupped her face and their lips touched.

"Oh, honey, that's wonderful news." She sounded happy, but the lines were still there. "What do I have to do?"

"Clean." He shrugged. "All you have to do is clean—"

"Who will look after the kids while I'm cleaning other people's houses?"

"Don't sound so disgusted, Agnes. It was either that or they find another couple who would do this, and I would be out of a job." He raised his voice.

Harris collected his model car and left the room with Stella following closely behind with her doll clasped in her arms.

He sighed, shaking his head. "I need the job, as you know."

Agnes nodded, but those lines were still prominently stuck on her forehead—the look of displeasure.

"This was the only job available. For six months, we'll live rent free in a lighthouse I'll need to care for, while you have a job cleaning the fifty houses on the isle. They want everything perfect for when the villagers return. It was either both of us or neither. The kids can help you, but only after their daily lessons and chores."

Agnes sighed irritably and didn't seem to care that Ben noticed.

He braced himself for an argument they had constantly —the *my father was right speech*.

Agnes closed her eyes.

He suspected she was counting to a hundred; counting to ten no longer worked.

When she opened her hazel eyes, they were smiling, and it was genuine—for once. Her creases were gone, and she visibly relaxed. "Okay, I know you're right. We can make this work. We can work out a schedule." She paced beside him with a finger tapping lightly on her full bottom lip. "The kids can do schoolwork in the morning after breakfast. After lunch, we can clean a house. If there are only fifty and we do one a day, it gives us plenty of time within those six months." She stopped in front of Ben, hands on her hips with an expression he could only decipher as determination. "You know, I wanted to yell at you. But I thought about it first, before opening my mouth. And you *are* right. We both need to pitch in if we're going to make anything work."

"That's my girl." Ben pulled her into an embrace, not knowing the full extent of what lay ahead for them.

Stella gripped her doll as the large rocks headed toward them. It wasn't the rocks moving but the ferry they were traveling on. They moved between the tips of the rocks once part of the mountain and stuck out of the water near the shore. Her mom and dad sat on the bench, whispering, while Harris played with his car on the far side of the ferry. She found a spot up front where the wind picked up the spray of the sea, and light drops fanned her face, leaving her lips salty when she licked them.

She watched the seagulls glide near the edge of the steep rock's edge, and some settled on parts of the protruding rock. From where she sat, the edge looked flat, but some ridges were wide enough for the seagulls to make nests and have babies.

As they floated past a dark sea cave, something smooth and shiny caught her eye. She squinted at the narrow opening between the rock's edge, but the ferry moved past, and she couldn't see it anymore. She wanted to tell her dad what it was, but she didn't have any words to explain.

Ben loaded the boxes of supplies onto his Datsun's back seat, with Stella and Harris squashed between. They drove the hour-long road toward the lighthouse and reached it while the sun was still out, but not for much longer.

Ben parked the car near the door and opened the trunk. "Let's carry what we can and settle in. I want to clean our sleeping area first before doing anything else."

"You finally made it," a man said as he walked around the car toward Ben.

Ben flinched at the sound of a foreign voice he wasn't expecting.

"I'm Tom." The man reached for a handshake. "Ah, that look on your face tells me nobody told you about me."

"No. They informed me no one else was here."

"I'm here," Tom guffawed, but it sounded forced.

"Am I at the wrong place?"

"No. You're at the right place. I was just ensuring this place is perfect for your arrival and to show you around."

"Alright." Ben glanced over his shoulder at Agnes, who shrugged in response. "Lead the way."

Tom walked with a limp. Ben couldn't discern which leg was injured, as Tom seemed to alternate his limp.

The family followed Tom up the lighthouse stairs while he rambled about the area.

"Have you manned a lighthouse before?" Tom asked, stealing a glance at Agnes. His roaming gaze travelled from her feet to her chest then eventually to her face.

"I have." Ben stood and scowled at Tom when he saw how he ogled his wife.

"Good. So you know what your generally duties are?"

"Yes."

"I'll tell you in any case. Perhaps your boy can learn a thing or two." Tom playfully nudged Harris with his elbow then faced Ben. "You're to keep the light and fog signal in perfect working order. Do you understand? Perfect. Working. Order. At night, you're required to keep a watch in the lightroom to ensure the light works properly. You cannot have a boat crash into the cliff here, or it's your ass." Tom smirked. "This isle doesn't have emergency services, and the community nurse is in hospital with the rest of the villagers. If anyone gets hurt, you need to sort yourself out or take your boat to the mainland. Understood?"

Ben nodded.

Tom continued with their tour, pointing at the various equipment and lights Ben needed to maintain. Finally, the tour ended in their sleeping quarters on the ground floor consisting of two rooms—one with a double bed, the other a bunk bed. There was one bathroom with a shower, and near the entrance was their kitchen.

They went outside and around the corner to a smaller shed.

"You'll need to start the generator when you need electricity, and, in the cupboard over there"—Tom pointed to a locked cupboard—"is gasoline, candles, and anything else you need to sustain yourselves. Here is the key." Tom handed Ben the key. "The firewood is in that cupboard over there." He pointed to another cupboard, this one without a lock.

They exited the shed and followed Tom to a bicycle leaning against the back end of the lighthouse.

"Do you cycle from one end of the isle to the other?"

"It's what keeps me alive and fit." Tom smiled, revealing sizeable gaps between his stained teeth. "Alright, I'm in town in case you need me. Good luck." He cycled away without looking back.

"That was odd," Agnes said as she latched onto Ben. "I'll make supper while you and the kids pack some stuff away."

Ben kissed the top of her head as he watched Tom cycle away until he blurred in the distance. He called the kids to help unload some luggage. He knew which box had the bedding, and he made the beds with Stella's help while Harris brought in their luggage.

By the time dinner was ready, the beds were made, and they had unpacked their clothing. They didn't have much of anything else, and they kept their furniture in storage until their six months were done. And, if they stayed longer, their furniture could stay where it was.

Ben checked the light upstairs to ensure everything was in working order before going to bed. Their first night on the isle was uneventful, with the soft whispers of the ocean song lulling them to sleep.

The next morning, Agnes made breakfast. Once everyone was done eating, they explored the area. They traversed down the path that led to the edge of the cliff they were on and descended the stairs to the tiny dock where a boat was kept for Ben to use to fish. When they reached it, the foul smell of decaying fish assaulted their noses, and they stopped before boarding the boat.

"Maybe take the kids back up," Ben said as he neared the boat.

"Come, kids," Agnes said as she backtracked, pulling the kids with her. "We're going back to explore the village rather. Come back up at lunchtime."

"Yeah, sure," Ben said absently, scanning the boat for the cause of the stench.

When he heard their footsteps fade, he boarded the boat. In one corner lay a heap of rotting fish, their bellies bursting with white worms, eyes popping with puss, and bone piercing what was left of their meat and scales. Birds and insects picked at what was left. Ben grabbed a stick off the floor and pushed the rotting fish overboard. He filled a bucket with sea water and washed the deck.

Once that was done, he ventured below. Someone had ransacked the small area. Life jackets, clothing, and books were strewn all over the floor like someone had tipped the boat upside down. He would clear it later. Back on top, he started the engine. It roared to life then cut out. He tried it again, and again, the engine roared awake then stalled as if something was stuck on the propeller.

Ben went to the stern and peered overboard. A net was caught in the blades. He reached into the dark water. The chill caught his breath, but he continued until his hand almost reached the net. Something moved and touched his hand. He pulled up his hand, biting back a scream. He glanced at the cliff to confirm his family was gone. He stared at the water, and whatever it was, was also gone.

It was only a fish.

With a shaky hand, he reached for the net again,

glancing at the water to his left then his right, and went deeper into the black waters.

The sun had cast a shadow over the boat and water, yet he still struggled to see anything. Water splashed before him, and he pulled his hand from the water again. He had to get a grip. He was near the ocean, and, if anything was splashing, it was only fish or seals or whales. He doubted sharks came this close. But still, it's only sea creatures.

Ben exhaled a shaky breath and tried to listen for anything, but all he heard was his heartbeat. Shaking the demons from his head, he reached for the net in one swift motion and pulled it out. He untangled it from the propeller and threw it inside the boat. He would see if he could fix it and use it again to catch fish.

Now that the net was out, he started the engine again, and it roared to life. He unhooked the rope and took the boat into the ocean.

Ben headed toward the skyline, pushing the engine as much as he could. The farther he went, the bluer the ocean became. The boat's engine sounded good now the net was untangled. When he was content, he turned back toward the isle. He stared in awe at the high cliffs where the lighthouse stood as he traversed the coastline. Water and wind whipped through his hair and on his skin, and it felt like the old days on his father's fishing trawler.

In the distance, he saw schools of fish and knew that could be one of the prime spots for him to fish. It was then he remembered he had to leave fish somewhere. He circled the boat around and headed toward the cliffs again. He drifted passed rocks that stuck out of the water. He couldn't see a place where he could leave the fish.

Ben remembered what his manager had said, that directly beneath the lighthouse, near the cliff, was a gloomy cave where he must leave the fish. His brows furrowed as he recalled the conversation yet couldn't understand what Preston had meant.

He floated passed the cliffs a third time and followed an invisible line downward from the lighthouse until his gaze met the water, and all he saw was thick darkness leading into the cliff. He headed for it. On instinct, he continued forward without stopping.

If someone didn't know what they were looking for, they would've missed it.

Ben entered a black, narrow water cave that branched into a maze of openings. He was grateful the boat was narrow enough to fit inside, or he would've gotten stuck. He made left turns, right turns, until he neared a platform atop a flat rock. He froze when he saw what stood there.

"You're late," it said.

Ben killed the engine and nothing else.

"I said, you are late. Now where's my fish?" It stood, peering down at Ben, its yellow beady eyes piercing daggers at him.

Ben blinked. His mouth was dry as he swallowed hard. When he finally spoke, all he said was, "I'm sorry."

"Sorry doesn't fill my stomach. Now get out and bring me fish. I've been waiting for four days for food. You know how hard it is on me if I don't eat. Or rather, how hard it will be on *you* if you don't feed *me*."

"What are you?" Ben finally found the words his mind was screaming.

It walked on two slithering tendrils across the flat rock until it was closer to the boat. "What do I look like?"

"I-I-I—"

"Come on. Spit it out."

"I don't know. I've never seen anything like you. Are you a boy or a girl?"

It laughed. The sound was like dangerous rolling thunder, leaning toward a baritone. "You're serious?"

Ben nodded.

"I take it they didn't explain anything to you?"

Ben shook his head. His mouth parted, and the cool air dried his throat. He was momentarily frozen. Only his eyes moved as he followed it. Its yellow eyes were large, surrounded by shades of green and yellow. A small bump sat in the middle of its face with three holes which Ben assumed was its nose. Its mouth was large, much like a fish's, stretching from one side of its head to the other with jagged teeth lining the top and bottom with multiple rows, like a shark. Its head was round, like a man, and it had shoulders, a waist, and tendrils for arms and legs. But its skin had a silver shine that changed color as it moved and, depending on how the light reflected, shimmering.

"Shame. Another poor sucker. You know, the last one was at least friendlier. I don't know what's wrong with you, but close your mouth. Don't you know it's rude to stare?"

Ben snapped his mouth closed.

"Fine. My name is Keeper. As to what I am, well, there's no definition unfortunately. I'm a combination of sorts." He winked. "But I protect *you* silly folks from the rest of *my* kind."

Ben's brows knitted together. "Why? What would your kind do to us?"

"Eat you," Keeper said sinisterly and smiled. The curve of his thick wet lips touched the sides of his head, and Ben was sure its entire face could open and swallow him whole.

Ben stepped backward and stumbled, landing on a wet spot.

"Yes, you're delicious, but I much prefer F-I-S-H. Now, go get me some." Keeper slithered back to where he had come from.

Ben started the engine and did what Keeper had commanded. He did not understand who or what the creature was, and, if what he said was true, they were food, unless he fished.

Ben found the school of fish he had seen earlier and fished them for an hour all the while contemplating the discovery of the monster-like creature. Keeper was tall like a man and spoke like a man, yet he was something completely different. Ben mumbled to himself how Keeper seemed like a human fishlike octopus, that he could possibly breathe underwater and as well as out of it. His head hurt thinking about what he had done, that he and his family were here and in danger. Was fish the only thing Keeper wanted to eat, or would he ask for something bloodier?

Ben shook the horror from his mind, but it didn't help. He eyed the fish flopping around and pictured himself and his family lying on deck, bloody, their guts spewing and flopping around, trying to get away.

If Agnes ever knew the truth, she would leave him for good. *My father was right*, echoed in his head.

He had put them all in danger, and Ben had to find a way out. He first needed to understand what exactly Keeper was and did before he could come up with any plan.

When he thought he had enough fish, he raced to the dark cavernous water openings and stopped where he had earlier. But Keeper was not there, and Ben killed the engine.

"Hello? Keeper?" Ben's heart raced as a cold sweat clung to his skin. His family was on this isle; he had intentionally brought them all to their deaths, and, while he was down here, they were all alone. He only hoped Keeper wouldn't hurt them.

"Coming," Keeper called out, sounding far away.

Ben offloaded the fish onto the rock's flat surface without exiting his boat in case he needed to make a quick exit.

A light, angry wind blew past Ben. When he turned around, Keeper stood before him and smiled gently—not like he had before. It was a small, thin smile that seemed to quiver.

"I'm sorry I frightened you earlier. That was wrong of me. I'm trying to change my ways, you see. I seem to have the nasty habit of being rude." Keeper flashed that same forced smile that looked painfully uncomfortable.

"Is this enough? If it's not, I can fish some more."

Keeper surveyed the pile of fish, and his smile broadened. "Hmm ..." He sucked air through his three nostrils and whistled. "*D-eee-licious.*"

The air snapped. Keeper disappeared and reappeared atop the flat rock, scoffing the fish into his large toothy mouth. He smacked his teeth together as he ripped through the fish, bones and all. Guts oozed from his mouth. He scooped that up too and sucked it down like it was spaghetti.

Ben gagged and glanced away quickly; a shudder ran through him as he heard the slurping, sucking, and splatting sounds of Keeper eating.

"Yes, just like that. Every two nights, I want a pile of fish. No more, no less, you see."

Ben turned around, and Keeper looked fuller, plumper, and much rounder than he had before and smiled lazily.

"No problem. I can do that for you. Is that all?"

"What's your name?" Keeper's expression seemed

genuine. He had no eyebrows, and his eyes were round orbs with nictitating membranes keeping them moist.

"Ben."

"And that's your lovely family up there, isn't it?" Keeper slowly licked his lips.

"Don't you—"

Keeper raised a webbed tendril with six smaller appendages for fingers. "I'm only kidding. Gosh, don't you like jokes?"

"Not when it comes to my family."

"So, that was in bad taste?" Keeper laughed, holding his fat belly as he enjoyed his own joke.

"Yeah, something like that," Ben said in a monotone and with a deadpan face.

"Fine, no jokes. Lighten up, Ben. You feed me, and I'll continue to protect your family and the rest of the stupid humans on this godforsaken planet." Keeper slithered into his room off to one side, leaving Ben standing on the boat.

He shook his head, unsure about the events of his strange day. But one thing he knew, he had to keep feeding Keeper. He didn't trust him, but he needed to keep his family safe all the same.

Stella was missing her daddy and wanted to show him the new dress Mommy had made for her doll. Mommy had said he was near the ocean in his boat, and she wanted to see where he was. She followed the path from the lighthouse to the edge of the cliff toward the sea and noticed a set of stairs hidden to her left. She descended the steep stairs until darkness swallowed her up, with the taste of the sea on her lips.

Stella reached the bottom and stepped onto a wet platform. Glancing up, she saw the stairs reach upward as if they went to Heaven—but she knew it only went to the lighthouse. She turned to see where she was. Squeezing her doll to her small chest, she followed the slippery path around the corner in the black cave. Light entered from the cave's mouth and bathed the water in a dark blue hue. Each wave that crashed against the foot path sent water into the air like magical dust, and, in each drop of water, she saw rainbows.

She heard her father's voice and walked faster to find him. She wanted to tell him she was a big girl and had come all on her own. She heard a boat start and then move away. She ran around the corner and saw her father's new boat disappear into the open sea. When she yelled, "Daddy!" he didn't hear her.

"Who's out there?" someone yelled.

"It's just me. Stella. What's your name?" Stella walked to where she had seen her dad's boat and stopped near the opening of another entryway.

The fish-man came out of its home. His slimy gills on the side of his neck opened and closed. His shiny skin changed from silver to blue, similar to that of soapy bubbles she liked to blow.

"You have very pretty colors." She reached to touch what she assumed was his arm.

"My name is Keeper. Was that your daddy?"

"Uh-huh."

"You shouldn't be down here. You could slip and fall into the water."

"I can swim, you know." Her little mouth tightened into a line for a moment until she surveyed him. "What are you? You don't look like us."

"I'm the keeper of this place. I stop those like me from coming into your world and destroying it. Would you like to see where I sleep?"

She nodded.

Keeper entered his room and beckoned her to follow.

Ben traversed the path to the lighthouse and heard a commotion ahead. He ran as fast as he could to find Agnes and Harris frantically searching their sleep quarters.

"What's wrong?"

"Did you see Stella on your way up?" Agnes asked as she lifted the mattress to look under the bunk bed. When she turned around, tears streaked her cheeks. "She was here a moment ago. I finished the dress for her doll—" Her mouth hung open. "The ocean! She wanted to show you the new dress. Oh, no." Agnes ran past Ben, who turned and followed her.

Ben and Agnes ran down the path toward the stairs leading directly to the boat. As they descended a step, Stella's head popped up on the other side.

"She's over there!" Ben pointed.

Agnes ran back up the stairs, passed Ben and darted toward Stella.

When Stella saw her family running toward her, she stopped. Agnes must've had an expression that scared Stella, because she started crying.

"Oh, it's okay, honey. I'm not angry. I was just worried. I thought something happened to you." Agnes lifted Stella and pressed her against her with all her strength. "Where were you?"

"I was looking for Daddy." Stella glanced at her father

with a knowing look. "I found these stairs that took me into the caves where Keeper sleeps."

Ben groaned inwardly. He hadn't wanted Agnes to learn about Keeper so soon. But, in order to keep Stella safe, perhaps it was the best time for Agnes to find out.

"Is he your imaginary friend?" Agnes asked.

"No, Mommy. He looks after us. Right, Daddy?"

Agnes glowered at Ben. "What is she talking about, Ben?"

"I didn't want to scare you. If you knew, we would've fought. I was worried you would want to leave the isle."

"What is down there, Ben?" Agnes folded her arms.

"It's okay, Mommy. He won't hurt us. He's protecting us."

Agnes ignored Stella and arched an eyebrow as she waited for Ben's reply.

"I don't know what he is, but he protects Earth from the rest of his kind. The only payment he needs from us is fish."

"That's why you fish?"

Ben nodded.

"Why didn't you tell me, Ben?" Agnes whimpered, raw emotions evident on her face.

"I'm sorry. I thought I was keeping us safe."

When Agnes didn't respond, Ben approached her like one would a skittish horse, gently pulling her into his arms. He didn't want the kids to hear what he was about to say. He leaned near her ear and said, "He's from another world, and he's keeping those like him from coming into our world and killing us. We feed him; he keeps us safe. It's a fair trade."

"Did you know this before coming here?"

He shook his head. "No, only that I had to fish, but I thought that was for someone else."

"Do you promise?"

"I promise." Ben kissed her temple. "I would never knowingly put my family in harm's way."

"If anything happens, promise me we will leave?"

"I swear." He held up two fingers.

"Daddy." Stella pulled on his shirt. "What about me?"

"Come here." Ben reached for Stella, and she extended her arms for him.

"Look, Daddy. She has a new dress." Stella beamed at him as she showed off her doll's new dress.

"It's beautiful. Promise me one thing, Stella, that you won't visit him ever again," Ben said as he walked with her toward the lighthouse.

"I'm a big girl."

"Promise Daddy you won't go there again."

"Okay, Daddy." After a moment, she added, "He took me to his home."

"What?" Ben almost yelled but stopped himself. "Did he do anything to you?"

"No." Her forehead crinkled. "He showed me where he sleeps, and there is so much stuff there. He collects treasures from the sea."

"Oh?"

"He says you mustn't forget to feed him."

"I won't. Promise me you won't go there again. Do you understand?"

She nodded but was unhappy about it. "He is very nice. And he has pretty colors."

"He might be nice at first, but we don't know what he can do to us. Or why he is here."

"He says he protects us."

Ben shrugged. "That's what he says. We don't know for sure."

After that day, Ben instructed Agnes to not allow Stella out of her sight.

Each day started with the family enjoying breakfast together, then Ben would leave to fish while Agnes took the children to clean the houses. They enjoyed a lunch together, then, while Agnes took delight in an afternoon filled with knitting or reading, Stella spent time with her father as he painted walls or fixed pipes or attended to any other general handiwork. But, on most days, Stella didn't go to her father, even though she said she had. She visited Keeper.

"Keeper, I've brought you something to try." Stella approached the opening to his little room inside the cave. She entered and found Keeper resting on his belly.

He jumped up in one swift motion and sat with his legs crossed and arms open wide. "What do you have for me today, little Stella?"

Stella opened her hands and handed him a slice of bread. "Mom baked it this morning. She says we don't have to clean a house today. I told Dad I'm with Mom and told Mom I'm with Dad so that I can visit you."

"You're going to get into trouble, young lass."

She giggled and sat across from him. "Go on, try it."

Keeper licked the slice of bread, his long slimy tongue flicking out and back in again. "My dear, this is like eating paper. It won't do."

Her bottom lip trembled, and tears welled in her eyes.

"Okay, just don't cry please." Keeper opened his mouth, his sharp teeth sparkling in the dim light, and took a small bite. He chewed once and swallowed. "Yuck." He threw the bread out of his room.

Stella giggled. "Okay, fine. No more bread for you."

"Just fish, Stella. The only food keeping me sated is fish."

Before Stella could respond, the roar of her dad's boat echoed in the room. She jumped up, ran out and disappeared around the corner. "See you tomorrow!"

On some days when Stella visited, Keeper told jokes; on other days, he played dolls with her and even showed her a few tricks. He would open and closed his gills on the side of his neck or would transform an arm into a large jagged knife that stretched to his room's entrance. His transfigured arm looked hard and full of deep cracks that seemed to glow green. She was in awe when he had showed her the first time. She even reached to touch it, but Keeper shook his head.

"Never touch a keeper when changed, or you too will become one of us."

That revelation shocked Stella, and she never dared try again.

She knew Keeper didn't want to scare her too much and would only show her the one arm that morphed into a large knife that sliced through rocks like butter and she was sure could destroy the lighthouse.

Every day she would tell Keeper how her previous evening had been and what she had eaten for dinner, and she would always leave before her dad arrived with Keeper's fish.

———

The family had been on the isle for a month when the earth shook. Stella left their home to visit Keeper, like she did every other day. She traversed the slippery path, and, just as she reached Keeper's room, she froze. It was empty.

The earth shuddered again, creating huge waves that crashed against the cave walls and spraying her with the salty water. Below her, objects in shades of purple, orange, and blue slithered just beneath the surface. The shapes moved from underneath the rock she stood on and through the cave's narrow pathways and into the open sea.

Stella continued on the path to see what the shapes were and walked until the path stopped near the mouth of the cave.

The earth cracked and shuddered. Stella lost her footing, gripped the rock and clung to it as more shapes moved in the murky waters beneath her.

"What are you doing here?" the voice she had heard many times before asked, only now it was deeper, commanding, and scarier.

Stella faced Keeper and screamed.

Keeper had transformed into the monster he had shown her before. But, instead of it only being his arm, his entire body looked like lava had flowed and hardened over time with hot blood moving beneath the surface. He grew larger as he took his full shape, and his yellow eyes shifted slightly sideways and widened. His mouth stretched bigger, showing more teeth. "Go home, Stella!"

Stella flinched.

He dove into the water and followed the shapes into the ocean.

Stella remained frozen as she watched the fight before her. Un-earthly tails splashed from the water, revealing a rainbow of smooth creatures that resembled what Keeper was before morphing into his bigger, scarier self.

Keeper rose from the ocean, his wide maw swallowing water and a creature in one great gulp. The colorful creatures attacked him at once, but they were no match for him.

They opened their tiny jaws compared to his massive one and nipped at his concrete skin. He swiped at them with the arm that resembled a jagged knife while the other arm was a great, enormous claw. With every attack on him, he grabbed one with his claw then sliced it in half, and a deep purple liquid spilt around them. Another attacked, then another, but Keeper was too great and powerful as he gripped the creature with his claw and squeezed it like clay out of his hand; this one had dark green blood and guts oozing from its mouth and ears. Keeper fought until all the shapes were dead and their bodies had sunk to the bottom of the ocean.

Stella stared at Keeper with wide eyes.

He noticed her, maneuvered toward her at a steady swim and stopped at the opening of the cave. "This is my true form, child." Keeper spun to reveal himself.

"You look like a big, scary mountain." She clenched her doll and wiped a tear with her free hand.

"Stella! Get away from him!" Ben yelled as he ran the same slippery path toward her. "What did you do to her?"

"Don't speak to me that way, human. I'm the one who saved your family from more of them." Keeper pointed to the darkest part of the waters inside the cave to where their blood had spilt. "When the earth shakes like it did today, that means those from my world have escaped and want to cross over. Do not tempt me to let them be!" His stony features glowed with moving streams of hot blood beneath. He softened as he shrunk to his usual slippery size and swam toward them. "And bring me my fish. I'm starving." When he reached the opening to his room, he added, "And don't bring her here again. Next time I see her, I will touch her, and, when that happens, she turns into something like me. Consider this your final warning, human." He disappeared into his room.

Stella burst into tears at Keeper's harsh words. But those words stuck to her like glue, and she would never forget them.

Ben fished for Keeper that afternoon and dumped the load near his room's entrance and waited.

"You can go," Keeper yelled from inside.

"You hurt my daughter's feelings. She was still crying when I left to fish."

"Good."

"You don't mean it!" Ben said a little louder, standing a little taller.

Keeper flew into Ben so quickly he didn't have time to stand his ground. Keeper gripped his throat and pushed him against the rocky wall.

"You can't touch me. I'll turn into you." He panicked.

Keeper smiled sinisterly, and his nictitating membranes flashed across his two yellow eyes. "I warned you, human. You can't tell me what to do."

"Did you hear what I said?"

"Don't care."

"Yes, you do. Beneath that hard exterior, you like us."

Keeper released Ben and stepped backward. He crouched near his food offering and bit into a fish with a ferocious hunger, cupping the blood and guts that spewed over, then drank from his hand. His eyes rolled into the back of his head as he savored every morsel. "I did her a favor, and you." Keeper finally looked up. "Now you don't have to worry about me eating her." He licked his wide lips.

"No, you won't." Somehow, he knew Keeper wouldn't hurt them. He was here to protect them. Ben turned on his heel. "I'll see you tomorrow with more fish."

Keeper grunted and feasted.

———

Ben returned every day with more fish, and every day he asked Keeper to apologize to Stella. Even though her tears became less and less as the days passed, Ben knew she was still sad. Keeper was from another world, yet, somehow, she had made him her friend against Ben's wishes.

Ben should've been happy that Stella wasn't visiting Keeper alone anymore, but he wasn't. And Keeper hardly spoke to him when he delivered the fish; all he did was grunt and eat. If Ben didn't know any better, he suspected Keeper had become somewhat depressed himself.

The days turned into weeks then months. Ships finally docked with villagers ready to return to their homes.

Agnes had cleaned each of the homes to perfection. Ben and his family greeted each villager as they came ashore.

That evening, the villagers invited Ben and his family to the town hall for a thank-you dinner.

Ben wasn't sure whether they knew about Keeper, so he would keep it to himself unless one of them raised the topic. When Ben didn't see Tom, he asked the leader why the other lighthouse keeper wasn't there to join the celebrations.

"There's only one lighthouse on this isle," the leader answered.

All these months, Ben had not ventured around the isle. He had stayed near the lighthouse to repair it, he fished in the nearby waters, and he spoke with Keeper; that was it.

He couldn't understand why he hadn't gone to the other side.

Not wanting to sound like a madman, Ben kept quiet about the issue and continued with the conversation about what had made them all so sick in the first place.

"The man who fished for Keeper, Tom, had wanted to leave the isle. Everybody begged him not to go, because we were afraid we couldn't replace him in time, since none of us could fish. Then, one day, Tom tried to poison us all with him. Luckily, we were helped in time. But, as you know, Tom didn't make it."

Ben's eyes widened as he remembered speaking to and shaking Tom's hand. He opened his mouth to ask more, but the leader asked, "How is our Keeper anyway? Behaving, I hope?"

"Uh, yes. I guess as well as expected." Ben scratched at his neck. Keeper had touched him months ago and had left a red welt around his neck that itched and was warm to the touch. Since then, Ben had tried not to scratch, but lately, it was becoming impossible not to.

The leader's laugh bubbled to the surface, and his entire body shook. "Yes, he can be a bit of a jackass, but we owe him our lives, you know."

Ben nodded. "Tell me, how did Keeper come to be here? And why does he care enough to protect us?"

"Well ..." The leader cocked his head and furrowed his brows. "I ... I can't remember." He turned to his wife. "Mavis, do you remember how Keeper came to our land?"

"Yes, he ..." The lines between her eyes deepened. "One day ..." She gasped and brought her hand to her mouth. "I can't remember."

The rest of the evening was just as strange as that conversation. The other villagers sounded drunk even though no alcohol was present. They had finished the food before he or his family had a chance to eat anything. They were all as strange as if he and his family had entered a foreign place.

As Ben and his family returned to the lighthouse, the conversation he'd shared with the leader swirled in his mind —the fact they couldn't remember how Keeper had come to be and Tom, the lighthouse keeper, was dead. All this seemed impossible, but then again, he couldn't explain Keeper either, therefore anything was possible on the isle.

Ben wanted to understand what was happening, and Keeper could answer his questions. He left his family at the lighthouse and descended the steep steps into the dark cave. The itch around Ben's neck intensified the closer he got to the cave.

"Keeper? Can we talk?" Ben asked near the opening of his room and tucked his hands into his pant pockets so he didn't scratch.

"What now, Ben? Haven't you seen enough of me?" Keeper's voice echoed around Ben, and he wasn't sure which direction Keeper was coming from. "I see the villagers are back," Keeper hissed near Ben's ear, making him cower.

"What happened to Tom?" Ben yelled, unsure of Keeper's position. As much as Ben wanted to know why the others couldn't remember why or how Keeper came to be, he needed to know about Tom first.

"Ah, scaredy-Tom. Let's just say he didn't like what he heard." Keeper appeared before Ben with a smile that cut through his face.

"What did you tell him?"

"Are you sure you want to know?" Keeper asked with a slimy expression that confused Ben; it seemed to Ben that

Keeper was mocking him. "Once you see, you cannot un-see." He warned.

"I want to know everything."

"Look around you, Ben. What do you see?" Keeper whispered sinisterly.

"What?" Ben shrugged then glanced around him. "We're in a cave, in a mountain near the sea."

"Look again." Keeper's voice was hollow and grave.

Ben scrutinized his surroundings. For the first time in months, he noted the green slime dripping down the ridges of the cave walls. Ben squinted at the wall, at something protruding from it—*skulls*. Ben backpedaled until his backside hit the wall, his head connecting with a protruding skull. He glanced at Keeper with wide eyes.

Water sprayed them. Ben licked his lips and tasted copper. He averted his eyes to the moving liquid below. Instead of the ocean, it was black ichor.

"Now you see it. Well, there's your answer. Tom asked as you just did, then he saw it and wanted off the isle. But I was afraid he would tell others what transpires here, and I couldn't have that. Once you see—I mean, truly see your surroundings—you're the only one who remembers. So, you, Ben, are the true lighthouse keeper of *my* isle."

Ben stared at Keeper as his mind reeled with his new reality. "What is this place? Are we dead?"

"It's still Earth, just a different Earth. My earth. Down there"—Keeper pointed at the black liquid below Ben's feet—"is a gateway where more of my kind are. Every now and then, some venture out. All this is true. But this is my isle that I keep monster free. I'm the only one who is allowed. This entire isle is another portal into my earth that I keep safe from your Earth."

"W-what does that mean for us?"

"Nothing has changed, Ben. You'll continue to fish and feed me while I keep everyone safe."

"And the villagers? How come they could leave and come back again? And why can't they remember."

"The only reason I allowed the other villagers to leave was because I wanted them alive and to return. I meant what I said, I want everyone alive and well, Ben. And that includes you and your family. Especially Stella." The gaze from Keeper's orbs flitted from Ben's eyes to his neck. "Is it itchy?"

"What did you do to me? It won't stop itching."

"It's because I touched you." Keeper sighed. "Wait here." He disappeared inside his room and returned a few seconds later. "Here, put this on." He handed Ben a shell filled with a slimy white substance.

Ben brought the shell to his nose and recoiled in disgust. "I'm not putting this stuff on. It smells awful."

"If you value your life, you will. Put it on before you really do turn into one of us."

Ben rubbed the foul fish-smelling slime all over his neck. The tingling sensation brought a burst of fire, then it disappeared, and his neck felt fine. There was no itch, no burn; there was nothing.

"Now, what?"

"Now, Ben, we carry on. You bring me fish for the rest of your life. The villagers stay happy and healthy while I keep the portal closed. And I keep your Earth safe."

FOUR

Alternative ending

The family had been on the isle for a month when the earth shook. Stella left their home to visit Keeper, like she did every other day. She traversed the slippery path and, just as she reached Keeper's room, she froze. It was empty.

The earth shuddered again, creating huge waves that crashed against the cave walls and spraying her with the salty water. Below her, objects in shades of purple, orange, and blue slithered just beneath the surface. The shapes moved from underneath the rock she stood on and through the narrow pathways of the caves and into the open sea.

Stella continued on the path to see what the shapes were and walked until the path stopped near the mouth of the cave.

The earth cracked and shuddered. Stella lost her footing, gripped the rock and clung to it as more shapes moved in the murky waters beneath her.

"What are you doing here?" the voice she had heard many times before asked, only now it was deeper, commanding, and scarier.

Stella faced Keeper and screamed.

Keeper had transformed into the beast he had shown her before. But, instead of it only being his arm, his entire body looked like lava had flowed and hardened over time with hot blood moving beneath the surface.

He grew larger as he took his full shape, and his yellow eyes shifted slightly sideways and widened. His mouth stretched bigger, showing more teeth. "Go home, Stella!"

Stella flinched.

Keeper dove into the water and followed the other shapes.

Stella didn't want to watch anymore; she didn't want to be around Keeper any longer. With her heart beating hard and fast, she turned and ran back the way she had come. Taking care not to slip, Stella dashed along the narrow path toward the stairs when a popping sound filled the surrounding air. With one hand on the railing, she turned to see what was out there. "Hello?" Her voice echoed in return.

The black water below swirled and splashed against the sides of the cave. The popping sound reverberated against the walls. When Stella glanced in the sound's direction, the water moved; something glided just below the surface she couldn't see. Something slithered fast as water splashed in its wake. It was heading in her direction.

Stella screamed, not wanting to wait for whatever was in the water. Her doll's dress caught on the hand railing and fell. She was torn between going down and fetching her doll or escaping. She glanced over her shoulder to see the darkness edging nearer and the something dragging her doll into the water. She knew she had to move and ran up the stairs as fast as her little legs could take her.

The popping sounded again.

But Stella didn't turn around; she didn't want to know what was out there, what lurked in the shadows of the murky water. Stella sprinted home as fast as she could. The lights were on, the front door was open, and she saw her parents searching for something. She dashed through the door, slammed it shut and pressed her tiny body against it. Realizing they could still open doors, she slid the lock in place.

"Stella!" Her dad ran down the stairs to her. "Where have you been? We've been looking for you."

Stella burst into tears when her father picked her up.

He tightened his arms around her shaking body, consoling her.

"Oh, baby, what happened?" her mom asked with her brother standing beside her, their expressions full of concern.

"I saw all of them," Stella said between gasps of air and tears. "More of them are out there, and Keeper scared me."

"Ben, we have to get off this place. You promised me if we were in danger, we could leave. We can stay with my parents for as long as possible. It's not safe here anymore."

As much as Ben hated the thought of staying with Agnes's parents, he had to accept this was the wrong place for them to be. His family was in trouble, and the longer they stayed, the worse it might become.

He nodded with determination. "Pack what you can. We're taking the boat to the mainland."

Each family member carried a bag with their personal possessions. If allowed, Ben would return to fetch their car and the rest of their items. But, right then, he didn't care;

he wanted his family safe and off the isle before Keeper realized they were leaving.

They neared the edge of the cliff and descended the stairs toward the fishing boat. The water had an inky likeness to it as the waves crested and fell.

"Quickly, get on." Ben ushered his family aboard, started the motor and steered them away from the cave and toward the mainland.

In the distance, Ben saw splashing, as if two whales were fighting, but Ben knew it wasn't whales; it wasn't anything from their world. What was out there was something completely out of this world, and he was relieved they were leaving.

More By N Gray

vinci-books.com/ulysses-exposed

I don't know who I am—but my enemies do.

I woke up with no memory, no powers—yet something inside me
is waking up. A vampire saved me. A were-leopard protects me.
But as my past resurfaces, I wonder: am I the hero... or the
monster they fear?

Turn the page for a free preview…

Ulysses Exposed: Chapter One

The air was cool, the sun warm against my face. I was sure it was evening in Sterling Meadow, and not daytime at the beach.

I pushed my fingers into the sand, but the hard concrete beneath shattered my dream. My eyes fluttered open. I was lying on cold ground, looking up at the dark night and the shiny stars scattered beautifully like diamonds across the sky. There were no clouds to ruin my view. It was peaceful and serene.

I glanced to my left, but an ache exploded at the back of my head, my blood trying to thump its way out. My eyes flitted to the sky once again. My pulse thundered in my ears, my eyes clouded over with dark swirls and stars of my own, forcing me to lay still for a breath.

When I lifted my left arm, I couldn't raise it any higher than my body before pain caught me in my ribs. I made a small yelping sound and lowered my arm back to the cold ground.

I raised my right arm, lifting it all the way to my head,

and felt something wet and sticky in my hair. Bringing my hand into view but there was no bright red; only the dark maroon liquid dripping from my fingertips.

I didn't remember much before I saw the stars in the night sky. I didn't remember how I got here, wherever here was.

With effort, I sat up, leaning on my right elbow, but my vision swirled and a headache blossomed. When I could focus again, I scanned my shadowy surroundings. A large dumpster was in front of me, full of garbage. Now that I could see it, I could also smell it. The stench wafted upon the air; the disposal trucks hadn't collected in a while.

Behind the dumpster was a brick wall with boxes on the floor and trash strewn around. It looked like an average alley, except it's not a place that anyone should lay in.

I tried to sit, my breathing now labored, but pain tore through my abdomen and flooded all the way to my toes. A soft cry escaped my mouth. Beads of sweat trickled down my face as I pushed with both arms until I was leaning against the wall. In a half-sitting, half-lying position, I slowly bent my knees and noticed that my jeans were ripped, a wound on my left thigh visibly oozing a dark, murky liquid.

It looked like claw marks. The only animal large enough to inflict a serious injury like this was a were-animal.

Were-animals had been living among humans for a while now; along with all the other monsters, vampires, witches, warlocks, fairies and dragons, to name just a few. We, the humans, tried not to be food for any of them, and there were laws protecting us against the monsters.

Being attacked by any were-animal, if it didn't kill me, could leave me infected with the viral strain or virus of that specific were-animal.

Shit!

If I survived—which was a big *'if'*—I would turn furry once a month when the moon was full. I didn't want *that* to happen. Nobody did.

I wiped sweat from my forehead and pulled the rest of my shirt out from the waistband of my jeans, looking to see why there was so much pain in my side. I wore a black vest beneath a black blouse, and the two pieces of clothing came out of my jeans easily as I pulled. Pain cut through my side again and I clenched my jaw. I lifted the two shirts higher, exposing my black bra, but as I was the only one there, there was no embarrassment necessary.

I froze when I saw an empty shoulder holster, a gun nowhere in sight. I hoped I had a license for the gun— humans got jail time for carrying a weapon without that piece of paper.

With both shirts pulled high, I saw the wound. There were small chunks of flesh missing from my left-hand side; the soft delicate meat between my hip bone and ribs was gone, chewed and swallowed by something with big teeth. The wound had tears splitting from it that almost reached my belly button, like the were-animal had wanted to rip me apart.

As I pressed gently on the wound, blood gushed thick and heavy from beneath my fingers, and the night sky swirled before me again.

When I came to a few seconds later, the wound was still trickling blood. If an organ had been nicked by the animal's teeth, there might not be enough time. If I was going to survive, I needed to do something quick.

I unbuttoned my blouse and steadily slipped it off my shoulders. With my teeth and hands, I tore the blouse in half, scrunched one half into a tight ball, and pressed it gently against the wound on my side. Tears began to trickle down my cheeks and onto my chest. I pulled the vest down to cover the wound and to hold the make-shift gauze in place. With the other half of the blouse, I flattened it out and twisted it so that it looked like a long rope and tied it around my thigh. It was the best I could do to stop the bleeding without having a belt.

With the tourniquet in place, a sharp, shooting pain vibrated up my spine and down to my toes as I secured the knot on my thigh, allowing me the freedom to hold the wound on my side closed with both hands.

I felt all the pain; the tearing of the bite wound and the pulling of the clawed wound as the adrenaline tapered off. I lay quietly, concentrating on my breathing and contemplating my next move.

I could scream for help and try to crawl out from the alley. But, there was a problem with that. I didn't think I would be able to move with this hole in my side, and I didn't know the neighborhood. There could be monsters leering around every corner, hungry to taste fresh human meat, and the moment they saw me they'd pounce. Vampires loved blood. Were-animals loved flesh. Witches could use me for their spells.

Shit.

My pulse hammered in my ears, and tiny sparks fluttered in my vision. I needed help. Now!

I sat straighter against the wall, my body positioned slightly to the right so that the wound on my left wasn't compromised. As I bent forward, something thicker than tears ran down my face. I'd been so concerned about the wounds on my leg and abdomen that I'd forgotten about the wound on my head. I wiped it away with the back of my hand to find more of the dark, thick liquid. This had to be the worst evening ever.

My breath caught in my throat when the sounds of men talking and footsteps nearing. They were almost at the opening of the alley. There was maybe three or four of them. I didn't know if they were good men and would help, or whether they would finish the job the were-animal had started. If they were vampires and saw all this blood, then I was the perfect victim. I hadn't heard of a vampire that could resist so much blood. And no were-animal could resist biting into fresh flesh. I was a *Happy Meal* to go.

But, I needed help urgently. I had to risk being discovered or I'd die a very slow, and painful death.

At first, I cried out softly. When they didn't respond, I cried out louder. The talking stopped, and the footsteps slowed down. I glanced over my right shoulder to see the entrance of the alley and rested my head; it was too much effort to keep my head up. In the light, I saw three of them, one slightly ahead of the others. They were staring at me.

Their eyes glowed like a cat's would when in the dark. The men were were-animals, and I was potentially vulnerable prey. The man in front, his face concealed in darkness, stood painfully still; possibly tempted at the dying woman on the ground.

I cried out again, this time a whimper, as the pain ripped through my body.

Grab your copy...
vinci-books.com/ulysses-exposed

About the Author

Multi-genre author writing twisted endings...

N Gray is a USA Today Bestselling Author who lives in Cape Town, South Africa, with her daughter and adopted cat named Miss Beans.

During the day, she's an analyst and provider profiler for a medical insurance company. At night, she types on her curved keyboard, creating fictional characters some may love and others you want to kill yourself.

She writes in four genres: urban fantasy, thriller, horror, and paranormal romance.

She now writes under Natalie Michaels for her new thrillers and SD Syns for her new horrors.